# THE CONTRARY DEBUTANTE

## The De Petras Saga, Book 3

## Emily E K Murdoch

## ARE YOU SIGNED UP FOR DRAGONBLADE'S BLOG?

You'll get the latest news and information on exclusive giveaways, exclusive excerpts, coming releases, sales, free books, cover reveals and more.

Check out our complete list of authors, too!

No spam, no junk. That's a promise!

### Sign Up Here

www.dragonbladepublishing.com

*Dearest Reader;*

*Thank you for your support of a small press. At Dragonblade Publishing, we strive to bring you the highest quality Historical Romance from some of the best authors in the business. Without your support, there is no 'us', so we sincerely hope you adore these stories and find some new favorite authors along the way.*

*Happy Reading!*

*CEO, Dragonblade Publishing*

# Additional Dragonblade books by Author Emily E K Murdoch

## The De Petras Saga
The Misplaced Husband (Book 1)
The Impoverished Dowry (Book 2)
The Contrary Debutante (Book 3)
The Determined Mistress (Book 4)
The Convenient Engagement (Book 5)

## The Governess Bureau Series
A Governess of Great Talents (Book 1)
A Governess of Discretion (Book 2)
A Governess of Many Languages (Book 3)
A Governess of Prodigious Skill (Book 4)
A Governess of Unusual Experience (Book 5)
A Governess of Wise Years (Book 6)

## Never The Bride Series
Always the Bridesmaid (Book 1)
Always the Chaperone (Book 2)
Always the Courtesan (Book 3)
Always the Best Friend (Book 4)
Always the Wallflower (Book 5)
Always the Bluestocking (Book 6)
Always the Rival (Book 7)
Always the Matchmaker (Book 8)
Always the Widow (Book 9)
Always the Rebel (Book 10)
Always the Mistress (Book 11)
Always the Second Choice (Book 12)
Always the Mistletoe (Novella)

**The Lyon's Den Connected World**
Always the Lyon Tamer

**Pirates of Britannia Series**
Always the High Seas

**De Wolfe Pack: The Series**
Whirlwind with a Wolfe

# CHAPTER ONE

*April 10, 1810*

"Oh, and the darling way she curled her hair!"

"One should not be only impressed by one's hair, Sapphy—"

"But did you not see the diamonds, Mama!"

Emerald smiled as she sat by the dying fire, the embers barely glowing in the drawing room of the de Petras home.

A quick glance at the grandfather clock in the corner told her it was past one o'clock in the morning. If it had not been for the marvelous book in her lap, she certainly would have disappeared off to bed hours ago, but, as it was, she had stayed up late enough to welcome her mother and sister back from a ball.

Emerald steeled herself for the following conversation. Curling up by the fire was, in her opinion, far superior to anything her sister could get up to. Sapphire certainly would not agree.

Captain, her faithful dog, was snoozing in her basket by the fire. Emerald watched her with a wry smile. No dances or balls for her. Goodness, what a perfectly quiet life—

The door burst open.

"Such diamonds as you never did see!" declared Sapphire happily.

Emerald's smile broadened. Her little sister, now fifteen years of age and in Society mere months, had a certain vigor and love of life that was infectious.

Opal de Petras, their mother, entered the drawing room wearily. "They were cut glass, I tell you Sapphy, no one could afford—"

"If Lady Romeril wore such things you would say they were real," said Sapphire, dropping her pelisse onto the pianoforte and launching herself onto the sofa. "I tell you, Ems, they were real!"

"They did glitter most impressively," admitted their mother, elegantly folding her wrap and placing it on a console table by the door. "But—"

"Oh, Ems, you should have come with us, the finery was simply spectacular!"

Emerald's smile faded. Well, she had expected the barrage of complaints about her lack of attendance, but to have launched into them so soon...

She swallowed before speaking softly. "I had no wish to go."

Sapphire twisted her head from her vantage point to look at her sister as she lay on the sofa and looked up at the ceiling. "Emerald de Petras, not wishing to go to a ball is the most confusing thing I have ever—"

"Tell your sister about the ball, do not berate her," their mother interrupted.

Emerald shot a grateful look at Opal, who was lowering herself into an armchair, groaning slightly as she took the weight off her legs.

If only she'd had the foresight to notice the time, to creep upstairs to bed where neither mother nor sister could tease her. Not that it was unusual. Emerald had not attended a ball for weeks, and only a few card parties. As for dinners...wild horses could not drag her there.

A curl of discomfort settled in her stomach as Emerald contemplated such a social occasion. All those people, all that noise, people watching her, judging her...

No. It was safest and calmest here, at home. There was nothing wrong with home.

Sapphire sighed, but there was little to douse her spirits. "Emerald, I have never seen so many feathers all in one room—I truly thought for a moment a bird from Africa had descended and was molting!"

"There were some very fashionable and very impressive people there," Opal admitted. "I was amazed the Duke of—"

"And I danced almost every single dance, except a country dance too dull for words, and Lady Romeril said I had my mother's spirit. Wasn't that nice!" said Sapphire impetuously.

Emerald caught her mother's eye and felt her cheeks flush.

*Her mother's spirit.* The scandal of their parents, their eventual remarriage, and the short time the de Petras children had spent living with Lady Romeril and her family were just stories to Sapphire.

But to Emerald, they were memories. Painful memories. Memories of loss, confusion, and pain. Her little sister had no idea what she was talking about.

*Their mother's spirit indeed,* Emerald thought wryly. It was hard to tell, without Lady Romeril before her, whether that was a compliment or an insult.

"And only one person had anything unkind to say about my stub," added Sapphire, raising her arms to the air and pulling off her gloves to reveal her arm which ended at the wrist. "And James gave him such what for—"

"Just the one?" interrupted Emerald, looking at their mother.

That was the trouble, wasn't it? Sapphire was so bright, blazing bright now their sister Coral's marriage enabled her to enter Society, that she was still innocent of the gossip's cruelty.

Anyone who was different, anyone who did not conform…

Emerald saw a flash of pain across her mother's face, then it was gone.

"Anyone who bothers to take the time to even be introduced to Sapphy can see she is naught but a mischievous girl with a temper," Opal said grandly, chuckling at her youngest's outraged expression. "Do not go and prove me right, Sapphy."

Sapphire relaxed, and Emerald relaxed slightly herself. The expected criticism had not come, for which she should be grateful. There was barely a day when she wasn't—

"You would have enjoyed it, Ems, if you had deigned to delight us with your presence," said Sapphire sharply. "Honestly, it was the most wonderful ball I've attended!"

"You said that about the last one," pointed out Emerald. *Truly, there was no one like her sister for hyperbole.* "And the one before that."

"I mean it this time," Sapphire declared.

Emerald shook her head wistfully. Was it because Sapphire was younger? Was it because she had been born different, that she had grown such a resilience? For there could not be two sisters more unalike. Sapphire was forward to the point of rudeness, whereas she…

"—and I spoke to almost everyone at the ball, I would be introduced, for I have waited years to be out in Society," Sapphire prattled on, "and everyone wished to know me, and at one time, I had at least fifty pairs of eyes on me!"

It was impossible not to shiver. Emerald could hardly think of anything worse. Fifty pairs of eyes—fifty people, all looking at her, staring at her, watching her, judging her?

Her stomach twisted again, this time more painfully. *It sounded awful.* She had certainly escaped a fate most awful by refusing to attend.

"I saw that."

Emerald's gaze snapped to her mother, who was frowning. "I beg your pardon?"

"I saw you shiver at the mere thought of attending the ball tonight," said Opal, her natural perceptiveness increased as it always did when it came to her daughters. "Emerald, you really must harden yourself to such occasions. When you marry—"

"I will not marry."

How many times, in how many variations, did she need to

say it?

Emerald had no wish for that sort of thing, no wish at all. Marriage? Constantly in someone else's presence, never alone? Being watched, being observed? Worse, the entire process that would lead up to a marriage, courting, judging, and being in public…

No. She was perfectly happy here with a book, living with her parents.

Sapphire groaned. "Not this again!"

"I was not the one who brought it up!" Emerald said defensively, tension spreading down her neck and across her shoulders. "It was Mama who said—"

"Marriage is to be expected, one cannot avoid the topic forever!"

Emerald sighed at her mother's words, louder than anything that had been uttered since they entered the room. Captain stirred by her feet, snuffling noisily, and she leaned to pick her up. The dog twisted in her lap, then settled.

Breathing slowing with the comforting weight of her pet, Emerald tried to calm herself. She was not going to win this argument at—what was it?—a quarter past one in the morning. No, the best thing she could do was retreat upstairs and put off the conversation for another day.

"I am tired," said Emerald firmly, aping a yawn. "I think I'll go up to—"

"—and I said they would not mind! Really, Edward, you worry too much!"

All eyes in the drawing room snapped to the door, which opened to reveal the third and eldest de Petras sister.

"See, I told you they would not mind," said Coral breezily, wafting in with a gracious smile. "Hullo Mama, I thought you'd be happy to host us for the evening, it's much too far for us to return to Glaenarm House, and—"

"What's wrong with your carriage?" asked Sapphire impertinently. "Hello Edward."

"Hello," said Coral's husband helplessly. "Apologies for intruding, I—"

"Oh, we're not intruding," said Coral, waving aside her husband's words with ease. "The carriage returned without us, a complete misunderstanding, but as you were so close…"

Emerald shrank back into her seat. *It was only Coral*, she told herself firmly, but her heart still pattered painfully with the growing number of people in the room.

Just Coral and her husband. They had been married months, after all. One would have thought she would be used to him.

"And where were you, Emerald?" Coral asked sharply as she stepped to the fire and sat opposite her. "I did not see hide nor hair of you at the ball, where were you? In the card room?"

"She," said Sapphire triumphantly, ignoring Emerald's begging eyes, "was not there!"

Emerald groaned as Coral's eyes sharpened. "Not there—you did not attend?"

"I am going to bed," said Emerald firmly.

Anything to escape this noise! Anything to escape the criticizing tongues, the assumption she had to be like half of Society and be desperately hunting a husband.

"How's Captain?" asked Edward, standing by the sofa.

Emerald tried to smile. It had been her brother-in-law who had gifted her the puppy. "Fine. I really do want to go to—"

"What's all this ruckus? Can't a man sleep in this place?"

The family turned to smile at the newcomer as Emerald groaned. Jasper de Petras, her father, had entered the drawing room, dressing gown wrapped around him and a smile on his face. It was now starting to become uncomfortably warm in here—or was that just her, those prickles of uneasy tension down her spine warming her beyond what she could endure?

"Oh, I am sorry to have disturbed you," said Opal with concern spread across her face. "See, Sapphire, I told you we should have gone straight to bed."

"And miss all this?" Sapphire looked, to Emerald's eyes, as

though she could not be more delighted that all the family—save Micah, of course, and their brother was so rarely at home—were here. "You're just in time, Papa, we're persuading Emerald to get married."

"Get married?" Their father raised an eyebrow and glanced at Emerald, who shrank back into her chair. "I was not aware Emerald had any interest in—"

"I do not!"

Emerald had not intended to shout. Raising her voice was a rare occurrence, one typically only to keep herself safe if a gentleman pushed past her most violently on the pavement.

But this was too much! She was tired, she had a sleeping dog in her lap, she wanted to run, hide, and get away from all this attention. She was not going to marry.

"Everyone wants you to be happy, Ems," said Coral.

Emerald glared. "And is matrimony the only way one reaches happiness?"

"Well, no, but—"

"What on earth is going on here?"

Everyone turned to the door. A tall, disheveled gentleman stood with a grin.

Sapphire squealed and jumped up from the sofa. "Micah!"

"Micah," said Jasper eagerly. "You're back, we haven't seen you for—"

"What are *you* doing here?"

Emerald could not understand Coral's coldness. Micah was here, the wayward brother, and that meant that the entire family was here. Here, talking about her.

Could she slip out through the parlor?

Just as Emerald rose, desperately hoping to avoid the inquisition which had started at such a late hour—or was it early?—Captain squealed in her arms at the surprise of being lifted so suddenly.

"Emerald, where are you going?"

Emerald sighed, her cheeks flushing and her heart pattering

painfully. Her family were truly good people, she had nothing against them—except their desire to see her wed…

"Ah, it's force Emerald to get married time, is it?" asked Micah impishly, settling on the sofa next to Sapphire and grinning. "Is it my turn to extol the virtues of marriage? I'm not sure I have many prepared."

Emerald had to smile at that. If there was a de Petras sibling who understood her reticence to marry, it was Micah—though for quite a different reason.

"Is the whole family against me, then?" she asked wearily, dropping into the armchair.

Her mother looked hurt. "Against you?"

"Against you?" Coral looked aghast. "How can you say such a thing? We are…"

Emerald allowed the words to wash over her. That was the trouble with living in a family where her mother, not her father, was the head of the household. There was so much more of a focus on matrimony, on children, on things Emerald refused to partake in!

"…we just want what's best for you," finished Coral.

Emerald swallowed. Sometimes the words she wished to say did not come to her, and half the time, she decided not to say them to keep the peace.

It was not a calm household. That was their Italian blood, according to their mother—though, in Emerald's mind, her father's stubbornness probably had something to do with it.

But this had gone on long enough. She was over the age of her majority, for goodness' sake! The sooner her family learned she was resolute in her decision not to marry, the better. Then she could just go back to reading, walking, and having absolutely nothing to do with Society in peace.

"Is it possible," Emerald said quietly, and the room hushed in a most disconcerting way, "that the best thing for me may not actually be marriage?"

As soon as the words left her mouth, Emerald knew she had

not convinced any of them.

Micah snorted, while Sapphire looked utterly perplexed. Coral looked a little offended, as though Emerald had personally attacked her, and Jasper shook his head as though Emerald should have known better.

She swallowed. Well, what was the point in having opinions if one was not going to share them? Was she not the best person to decide what would make her happy?

Captain snuffled in her lap, and Emerald's gaze dropped to the dog beneath her hands. Captain did not care whether she was wed or not. Captain could care less if she was on the marriage market or never left the house.

No, all the dog wanted was a warm place to sleep and more scraps than were good for her.

Emerald sighed. An easy life. Something to be admired.

"I do not understand you," Sapphire was saying. "Not wanting to get married? When there are so many handsome gentlemen out there just waiting to—"

"Sapphy!"

The cry of censure came from almost all directions, and Emerald could not help but smile as the conversation drifted toward her youngest sister and her inappropriate language.

Only her brother did not join in. Emerald tried to catch his eye, certain Micah would stand by her side. After all, her brother was far more interested in mistresses, was he not, than actually marrying?

Despite her best efforts, Micah did not look at her.

Why, Coral had received almost twenty proposals before she accepted Edward. Could she not be married enough for the rest of them?

"Emerald, you cannot lock yourself away in here," said Opal sternly.

Emerald jumped. She had not noticed the family had ceased their conversation with Sapphire—and her cheeks burned as all eyes returned to her again.

"The Season is almost over," she said weakly. "I do not believe I am much missed by anyone of consequence—"

"We missed you!"

"In the *ton*, then," Emerald added, glaring at Coral. Why was her sister not on her side? "And then the nobility can disappear off to their country estates and leave me in peace."

"But—"

"I think we can find a compromise," said her mother over Coral's protestations.

Emerald blinked. *A compromise?* A compromise had never been offered before. In truth, she was not entirely sure what a compromise would look like. An engagement that was never fulfilled?

"What do you mean," she said wearily, exhaustion tugging her eyes, "a compromise?"

All eyes were on Opal now, to Emerald's great relief, but then she saw the slow and rather satisfied smile on her mother's face. That did not bode well.

"An arrangement between us," said Opal. "That you will attend ten balls—there cannot be more than ten left this Season. After that, we will never demand you attend a ball again, or a card party or a dinner, anything like that."

Emerald stared. *Never again?* Never hear the complaints and moans that she spent too much time on her own, never hear the criticism that she was a wallflower, a loner? Never be forced to dress up and parade around in a ballroom?

"Ten balls, that is all." Her mother was examining her closely. "What harm could they do?"

The silence in the de Petras drawing room was absolute, save for the snores of Captain in Emerald's lap.

*Ten balls. What harm could they do?*

The thought of one ball was enough to spark panic in Emerald's heart. Any ball was a difficult experience, one fraught with tension and awkwardness and embarrassment.

But to only have to endure ten more in her life…to be free,

after that, of familial obligation? In short, to be permitted to hold to her resolve to never marry?

Emerald's gaze had dropped to her dog, but it lifted now to examine her mother, who was smiling benevolently.

It all seemed too much like a trick…but Emerald could not see any way her mother could make the balls any more excruciating than they already were. And then she would be free.

It would be worth it, she decided, her heart skipping a beat.

"Ten balls," Emerald repeated slowly.

Micah looked up and caught her eye but said nothing.

"But Mama—"

"Coral, I know my business," said Opal firmly. "So, Emerald. Is it a deal?"

Emerald took a deep breath. "Ten balls. Well, it's not as though there is any possibility of meeting a gentleman I actually wish to marry in merely ten balls, is there? I accept."

# CHAPTER TWO

*April 15, 1810*

Robert Ainsworth, Marquess of Swindmore, glared at the door before him.

He had no memory of getting here, but that was no surprise. How many times over the last six months had he made this journey? Over and over again, his footsteps taking him along the same London streets, the same lane that acted as a shortcut, the same path no matter the weather or time of day. The entire thing was now rather automatic.

Today was the last time.

The brisk spring air chilled him slightly. Robert wished to goodness he had thought to put a greatcoat on, but he had an engagement straight after this one that would not brook anything so unfashionable as a greatcoat.

No, he would spend a little time in here, finishing what he started—or at least, what was started for him—six months ago, and then it would be over.

He would never have to come to Parker, Bells, and Hamble again.

Drawing a deep breath as the sun started to dip below the London horizon, Robert knocked briskly on the door. The knocker was brass, highly polished, as one would expect at a solicitors' office.

Oh, if only he did not have to do this. Robert had considered, many times the last few weeks especially, calling the whole thing off.

There was surely a different way around this, another solution to the problem he had not already considered. Wasn't there? Surely this could not be the only option available to him.

The last resort of a desperate man.

A footman opened the door and bowed. Robert grimaced and stepped forward.

He had no time for niceties. The sooner he could be in, done, and out, the better.

"My lord," the footman muttered, bowing as the marquess passed him in the corridor. "Mr. Hamble is—"

"I know the way," said Robert darkly, as though admitting a terrible personal fault. *Well, was it not, in a way?* How many gentlemen of his rank knew so intimately the inside of a solicitor's office? "He is expecting me."

The appointment had been made a week ago. Robert had thought that just far enough to prevent him from thinking about it overly much, and yet just close enough that he could not be accused of putting it off.

And now it was here. After all his hopes that a reconciliation could take place, that they could finally be brought to understand each other—*that she could be brought to reason*, he thought darkly as he stomped up the staircase—it had come to this.

His heart twisted painfully as Robert pushed open the door to Mr. Hamble's office. Everything within him railed against the decision he would, officially, be making this evening, but he would be a fool to leave the business unfinished.

No, the moment she had shouted at him the truth and the scales had fallen from his eyes, leaving Robert in no uncertain terms as the injured party…

He had been forced to take this action. She had forced him.

Robert swallowed, ensuring a polite expression was on his

face as the gentleman rose from behind a desk. "Mr. Hamble."

"Your lordship," said Mr. Hamble sagely, though with a slightly irritating smile Robert did not like. "You are punctual."

"I am always punctual," snapped Robert.

He regretted it immediately. What kind of cad was he, that he would respond to such a polite banality with such force?

Besides, he was always punctual, but he did not have to declare it. Only fools demanded to be respected for the basics of civility.

"Well, I did think you may perhaps forget this appointment, as you forgot the last one," said the solicitor delicately, though there was still a smile on the older gentleman's face that Robert did not like. "One would almost think you had no wish to go through with it."

Robert sat heavily on the chair opposite the desk without being invited. "One might think that. But one would be wrong."

"Naturally," said Mr. Hamble quietly, resuming his own seat.

Silence fell between them, a silence Robert was determined to fill if only he could think of something half rational to say. Rational was not a word that could be used to describe him today.

How had, after two years of seemingly happy marriage, had it come to this?

*"You'll never be like him,"* she had taunted that terrible evening when the truth had been revealed. *"Never."*

*"You don't know what you're talking about!"* he had shot back, his heart breaking, unable to take in what she was saying. *"You don't know what you're about to lose, what you're about to give up!"*

*"What, you?"* A terrible smirk had spread across her face, that beautiful face he knew so well. *"You'd never have the guts to do anything about it, Robert. You're no true Swindmore, you've not got the bravery to do anything about it. I'm your wife, after all..."*

Robert's hands clenched into unconscious fists. It had not been his doing, not his will to walk this path, but she had done nothing but force him. But that was not his solicitor's fault.

Mr. Hamble may find the whole thing amusing, but he had been careful with the paperwork and, as far as Robert could tell, discreet.

*And that was the important thing, wasn't it?*

Robert swallowed, tasting bile in his throat. The last thing he wanted was for Society to hear about all this. Oh no, as far as they knew, he was a free man.

This was the last step on a painful journey.

Then he could pretend the whole damned thing had never happened.

"I have it here," said Mr. Hamble abruptly. "I assume you've not changed your mind?"

Robert attempted to stay calm. "No."

It was not his mind that needed to be changed. It was not his behavior that had brought them here, not his decisions that had broken sacred vows, killed faith.

Mr. Hamble delicately brought out a piece of paper from a draw. It was covered in scrawling writing in a hand designed for complexity, not clarity. There were a number of large *X's* along the side, alongside thick lines which were evidently designed for signatures. Some of those lines already held a name.

Robert's stomach lurched. Even upside down and across the desk, he could recognize her handwriting anywhere. Large swoops and whorls, all elegance and decorum.

Such a shame that did not extend to her character.

"All of the official parts have been completed, of course, I have taken the liberty of doing that for you, my lord," came the quiet patter from the solicitor. "In these cases, it is generally simpler to ensure…"

His voice became a low buzz in Robert's ears. He had no interest in the details, only the end result, one which was hard to comprehend. But her bedchamber was already emptied, the stable no longer held her mare, and though he sometimes reached out for her in the night, she was gone.

Almost completely.

"I have a pen here ready for you," said Mr. Hamble quietly, turning the sheet of paper around and pushing it toward him.

Robert leaned forward to the desk, reaching for the pen which felt heavy in his hand, as though it were made of lead, not wood. His eyes danced across the lines on the paper before him, attempting to take it all in but struggling to read a single word.

*This was it.* Paperwork and court hearings, discreet petitions to royals, and a most shameful private discussion in the House of Lords...

And here they were. Just one piece of paper, a few scattered signatures separating him from marriage and bachelorhood.

How was it possible that within a moment it could end? It was impossible to fathom. It was repellent.

But staying in the marriage, knowing what he did now...that was just as impossible.

"Having second thoughts, my lord?"

Robert's gaze snapped up. *The impertinence of the man!* "No."

He had spoken coldly but not entirely truthfully. At the end of the day, one did not wed a woman with the expectation it would end in barely hidden scandal. Thank goodness they had met abroad, married there, and spent most of their time in the north. London Society had heard nothing of his marriage, and they would hear less of his divorce. Not that he could be blamed.

She had been the one to betray him. She had been unfaithful, had laughed in his face when he had asked why she had not kept to their marriage bed.

Robert hardened his heart. He would no longer permit that— that woman!—to hold the Ainsworth name. He would be without a marchioness, true, but better that than being saddled with the one he had.

Before she fell with child and attempted to pretend it was his own...

Dipping the pen in the proffered ink well, Robert took his time to elegantly, and with perhaps even more refinement than usual, sign his name at each place where an X awaited it.

*Swindmore.*

*Swindmore.*

*Swindmore.*

*Swindmore.*

*Swindmore.*

And it was done.

Only when Robert placed the pen back on the desk, ignoring the splot of ink it left there, did he realize he had been holding his breath.

*It was done.* He had signed it. After putting it off for so long, after knowing there was no way back once he had done such a thing, it was done.

"Well done, my lord," said Mr. Hamble in that horrible smarmy way he had. "You are officially divorced."

And he was officially no longer required to interact with such a man. No more paperwork, no more meetings, no more discussions about property and money and whether or not she could counter-sue him.

As though she had any evidence of his misconduct. It was an outrage to suggest it.

But the news that he was, once again, a bachelor, did not spark any joy within Robert's heart. Quite the contrary, it was impossible not to feel an element of regret. Of sadness. Loss of the marriage he had been sure he would have.

The solicitor pulled the paper back to him, examined it quickly as though Robert may have forgotten how to spell his own name halfway down the page, and nodded.

"Excellent, I can file that now everyone…ahem, involved, has seen it," he said quietly, depositing it in a drawer in his desk.

Robert tried to smile, his jaw tight. *Everyone involved.* That was one thing he should applaud his solicitor for, he supposed. The man had never mentioned that woman's name in his hearing, and for that, he would be forever thankful.

It was bad enough he was still receiving bills for her expensive habits; modistes, haberdashers, even a patisserie had attempted to force him to pay some inordinately large costs.

Well, no longer. Isabelle was no longer his wife. She had taken another man into her bed, and Robert had now cut all ties. She would now have to lie in the bed she had made.

"Congratulations," said Mr. Hamble, leaning back in his chair. "Or I suppose, commiserations."

A barb of pure agony wrenched through Robert's heart. If he had known, even a year ago, what 1810 would entail…

Well, he would hardly have believed it. They were so happy—they had been so happy. But that was all over now.

Steeling his heart and hoping his voice would be steady, Robert said, "No, I believe I am to be congratulated. I have extricated myself from a treacherous wife. I am free."

He regretted the instant of vulnerable honesty at once. Swindmores did not speak of such things, particularly to strangers, and Mr. Hamble could still be considered a stranger.

Why, he had known him but for half a year. Robert had not wished to bring this matter to the family solicitors. He could not bear to look into the face of Michaels, whose father and grandfather had served Swindmores from time immemorial.

No, this particularly shameful matter had been taken to another solicitor, and that meant Robert would be well advised to hold his tongue.

"There is nothing to be ashamed of, my lord."

Robert looked up sharply. Mr. Hamble's voice was gentle, far less infuriating than when he had stepped into the office just minutes ago. *Was that…sympathy…in the man's eyes?*

"Try telling that to the *ton*."

"Some marriages do not work, it has happened for generations, my lord," said the solicitor quietly. "Trust me. There is no fault apportioned to you—"

"I should think not!" Robert attempted not to speak hotly, but he was sorely provoked. *Fault?* How on earth could this disaster be considered his fault!

"Fault was not quite the right word," Mr. Hamble said hastily. "I meant...well. There are several divorced people within Society now. Times are changing. This is the nineteenth century, after all."

Robert shrugged, preferring that to a vocal opinion. Yes, it was true, divorce was starting to become—not commonplace, certainly, but no longer rare.

Gritting his teeth, Robert attempted to push away the shame that rose, unbidden, into his heart. Perhaps if he had been a better husband, a more attentive lover—

But no, he could not think that. No one could go back and change things. He had to look to the future. He had to think about what was to come.

Robert groaned under his breath. *That damned ball.* He had almost forgotten his commitment. Well, he would have to put in an appearance.

"Well, if that is all, my lord..." said the solicitor delicately, his voice trailing off.

Robert rose to his feet. "That is all."

Mr. Hamble rose, too, offering his hand. "It was an honor to serve, my lord, and I hope if you are ever in need of such support again—"

"I do not believe it likely I will be marrying again, let alone seeking another divorce, Mr. Hamble," said Robert cuttingly. *Really, the manners of the man!*

The solicitor's cheeks reddened, and he dropped his hand. "Of course, I did not mean to imply—"

"I say good evening to you," Robert said sharply, glaring. The sooner he could be out of here, the better.

"Yes, good even—"

The marquess had already turned and swept out of the room, slamming the door behind him in a pique of anger that did not reflect well on him. By the time Robert had reached the bottom of the stairs, regret had already entered his heart.

Perhaps he should not have been so harsh. It could not be easy, acting in such business and finding the correct words. Lord knew Robert himself was never one for carefully parceling his thoughts into appropriately consumable phrases.

There was a reason he had such few acquaintances in Town.

But as he strode along the corridor, the footman bowing low as he opened the door, Robert knew he could at least congratulate himself on having done the darned thing.

"Good night, my lord," murmured the footman.

Robert just nodded. He stepped out into the cold air, took a deep breath, and looked up at the moon, rising over the Houses of Parliament in the distance.

The first time he had looked on the moon as a free man.

"Free man," he muttered as the door snapped shut behind him. "Free!"

He'd never be free. Never free from her, from the way she looked at him, that smile that turned his stomach, the way she coaxed pleasure from him …

No, he could not think that way. She had betrayed him and was no longer his wife.

Robert glanced along the street. It was relatively quiet, a few carriages meandering on their way to evening engagements, no doubt. Though every fiber of his being craved for the silence and solitude of his own peaceful study—perhaps with a glass of brandy and a cigar, his own celebration of the end of such matters—he had, rather foolishly agreed to attend old Orrinshire's ball that evening.

Well. Attend was perhaps too strong a word. Putting in an appearance was more like it.

*Go in*, thought Robert as he started to stride down the street, *make a fuss of the host, make sure to lose a loud round of cards so everyone would recall he was there…then retreat.*

Back into the quiet of his own home.

He sighed heavily. Well, perhaps he could make it more interesting. Perhaps there was a way to entertain himself, even if the rest of Society was going to be unbearably dull.

A small smile crept across his lips as Robert turned a corner.

He could find a young miss and seduce her. Get some of this tension out of his system.

Well, why not? He had needs like any gentleman, and with Isabelle now out of his bed, out of his home, out of his life, he was in need of a little pleasure.

Yes, he would find a young miss just desperate for the plucking and make it his business to seduce her. After all, it was not as though anything else interesting could happen at a ball.

# CHAPTER THREE

*April 17, 1810*

*T*HE FIRST BALL.

Emerald could feel every inch of her skin. It was a strange thought that pattered through her mind when she had first entered the de Petras carriage, Sapphire chattering away as though this was the most exciting thing to ever happen.

When she had sat in that carriage, Sapphire to her left, her mother opposite, Emerald had been certain her entire skin was red, flushed. It was certainly hot.

"But you look lovely, my dear," said Opal genially. "I must say, I am glad to see you are keeping up your side of the bargain."

Emerald had attempted to smile as the carriage pulled away. "My side?"

"Well, you have not just thrown on the oldest gown you could find, pinned your hair, and called yourself ready," said her mother with pride in her voice. "You know what is expected of you as a de Petras."

*What is expected of her.* Well, Emerald could not deny she was perfectly aware what her mother hoped for this evening. To decorate herself lavishly, cover herself with jewels, stride into the Duchess of Orrinshire's ball, dance with one gentleman, make him fall in love with her, and announce their proposal before the night was over.

She smiled painfully. "I have tried, Mama."

And she had, no matter how ridiculous the expectations. Emerald had chosen her favorite gown—light green with ruffles, sleeves that fell to her elbow then flared with lace, gentle ruffles down the bodice.

It was not the height of fashion, to be sure, but her mother's lady's maid had done her best with her hair, and she was wearing her favorite emerald and pearl necklace with matching earbobs.

"Lord, I don't know when I have seen you so impressive," said Sapphire with a grin. "You almost look as though you might enjoy yourself!"

"Well, I won't," said Emerald, just softly enough for their mother not to hear.

Even so, she flushed as though she'd been overheard. It was most difficult, hating crowds in a family that seemed to do nothing but attract attention. If only they were not so different, if only there were not so much scandal in their past.

Emerald sighed and looked out the window, though it was too dark to see a thing save flashes of light as the carriage rattled down streets and past windows.

*All she had to do was attend a ball,* she told herself sternly. *Well. Ten balls.*

But only one tonight. She could stand there, talking to no one, not dancing, not playing cards. She would have to consider it a game. A game, that was all. How long could she go without speaking to anyone? Without catching anyone's eye. Without embarrassing herself or being embarrassed.

"Sapphy, careful!"

"Are we there?" said Sapphire eagerly, throwing herself across the carriage to peer up through the window at the place where they had halted.

Emerald forced her sister off her lap. "I think so."

"And not before time, too," said their mother, patting her hair and spreading out her fan, fluttering it before her. "I would hate to be late."

Sapphire rolled her eyes. "Mama, we won't be the last to arrive, I can tell you that!"

A slither of curiosity peaked in Emerald's heart. Sapphire had only been out in Society a few months, hadn't she? How was it possible that she understood all the vagaries of the *ton,* something that Emerald had struggled with since she was forced into company?

"How do you know?" she asked as a footman reached out to open the carriage door.

Sapphire giggled. "Why, Lady Romeril is always at least three hours late, isn't she, and she always says everyone else is too eager."

Emerald caught her mother's smile. It was probably fortunate for all their sakes that Lady Romeril was friends with Opal de Petras, or they would all feel the edge of her cutting tongue.

"Now, Emerald, you must dance with—"

"That was not the agreement," cut in Emerald sharply as her mother was helped out of the carriage.

Her heart thumped painfully as she tried not to think about dancing with a complete stranger at a ball. Everyone staring, gossiping about her, trying to guess his intentions toward her...

"Oh. I suppose it was not," said Opal disappointedly as Emerald was helped out of the carriage by the footman. "I suppose we could always add to—"

"Absolutely not," said Emerald firmly, though her voice faltered as she straightened up and smoothed her skirts.

There were so many people here. The street was absolutely teeming with guests of the Orrinshires, a blur of faces and chatter, laughter as people entered the house, so much noise...

Her thoughts started to swirl, as though the very ground she stood on was shaking. Her breathing tightened, her chest was rigid, her breath tight—

"Mama, you cannot change the compromise on Ems just like that," came the sympathetic voice of Sapphire as her head appeared at the carriage door. "Thank you."

The youngest de Petras stepped onto the pavement and beamed up at her mother and sister, looking round with wide eyes at the spectacle.

Emerald watched her. It was difficult not to be envious of Sapphire. Several years younger, yes, and without some of the elegance and grace of her older sisters…but still. Emerald had to admit there was something remarkably powerful about her boldness.

Why, the girl had entered life with laughter and no shame whatsoever and did not appear to be changing in the slightest as she went through the world. No matter what happened, Sapphire met it with a smile.

It was not seemly to be so envious.

"Ready?"

Emerald swallowed at her mother's question. "Ready for what?"

Opal blinked. "Why, to go in, of course."

Emerald hesitated. *Ready?* She had never felt less ready, though, perhaps, her very first ball was more frightening than this. She'd had no idea what to expect, and it had fatigued her greatly. The constant same three questions she had to answer over and over again, her name, her age, and whether she would dance.

The same three answers.

Sapphire giggled as she slid her arm into her sister's. "Goodness, it's almost like you are a debutante all over again!"

"A contrary debutante," said their mother wryly.

Emerald flushed. "I wanted to stay home. If I am to embarrass you, I could return—"

"Not so fast," Opal said hurriedly, pulling her daughter along.

"The sooner we can leave," Emerald said with a wry smile, heart pattering painfully.

It was the phrase she and her mother had concocted when she had first entered Society. Her anxiety at any ball, every ball, had been expected by the family but even Emerald had been astonished at how…how afraid she had been.

Those same feelings were returning as the three de Petras women walked up the steps into the warmth and light of the Orrinshire home.

Emerald swallowed. She could not breathe. She was not getting enough air, but that made no sense, for her chest was rising and falling, faster and faster, yet there was no breath in her lungs—

"Your pelisse?"

Emerald shrank back from the speaker behind her, whirling around. "No!"

"Emerald, give the nice man your pelisse," said Opal quietly.

Blinking, Emerald saw it was no attacker lurking behind her but a footman in the Orrinshire livery. He stared, slightly bemused, as she removed her pelisse and thrust it at him, keeping as far from him as possible.

They were only in the hall, a few people chattering away in a corner. Emerald's gaze dropped to her hands, folded before her.

*Oh, this is intolerable.* How had she thought she could survive attending not one, but ten of these over the next few months?

"Come on, girls," said Opal quietly.

Emerald looked up, pleading silently that her mother would permit her to return home. Surely it was clear this compromise was not going to work.

But Sapphire slipped her arm once again into her sister's. "You'll enjoy it, I promise."

It was not the lighthearted, foolish tone Emerald had come to expect, but a gentle one.

Emerald swallowed, tried to nod, realized she could control either her head or her feet but not both, and concentrated on putting one foot before the other.

Taking her inexorably toward the large double doors.

"Ready?"

Try as she might, Emerald could not speak, could not say she was certainly not ready, would never be ready, wished quite heartily to go home and—

"The de Petrases!"

The loud booming voice of the announcer made Emerald wince, but it was nothing to the embarrassment of all eyes in the ballroom turning as they stepped into the room.

It was bright. Dazzling. It could be the numerous candles or the many diamonds—or perhaps it was the hundreds of eyes that had just turned to look at them.

"Mama," Emerald breathed.

She had not moved. Her feet were frozen to the ground, and Sapphire was jerked back as she tried eagerly to rush forward.

Emerald's heart was beating so quickly now, she could hardly hear it, a mere purr in her chest. She tried to swallow but could not move her tongue. Her head was spinning. This was a nightmare, a nightmare from which she could not wake—

"There we go," came a gentle voice.

Her mother took Emerald's other arm, and she found herself slowly moved into the room and then immediately to the left, where there was a quiet corner.

It was as though she had lost a few minutes of time. The chattering buzz of a ball had returned, people turning back to their friends and talking about her. Or not about her. She could not tell.

She blinked. Sapphire and their mother came into view.

"Emerald?" said Sapphire nervously.

Emerald tried to smile. How long had it been since Sapphire and she had both attended the same ball? Now she came to think of it, she could not recall that they ever had. Which meant this was the first time her sister had seen her like this, unable to move as fear overswept her.

"She'll be quite well in a moment," Opal's calming voice said, and Emerald did not have the strength to disagree. "You stand with her here for a moment, Sapphy, while I go and make a sweep of the place."

"Mama—"

But her mother was gone before Emerald could say any more.

She looked helplessly at her sister. "Y-You must think me a-a dreadful fool—"

"I think you and I are very different," interrupted Sapphire, her voice low. "But different is not bad. We are de Petrases."

A warm sense of relief poured through Emerald's bones, and her joints became unstuck. She took in a deep breath and found to her relief that her headache started to dissipate now she was breathing again.

"We'll just stand here for a moment," Sapphire said cheerfully as the room continued to fill up and a gaggle of gentlemen stood beside them, laughing away at something one of them had said. "And then we can dance. Which gentleman do you want?"

"Sapphy!"

Emerald could hardly believe it. How did she do it, stand there, making such bold statements? Or was it she who was the strange one? Everyone else seemed to be enjoying themselves, after all. Some people longed for balls in the same way she craved solitude. Why, she could well remember the fuss Sapphire had made when Coral had been unmarried, and the youngest de Petras had not been permitted to come out into Society.

"—rather pretty ladies here tonight too, though I say so myself," one of the gentlemen in the group beside them said in a lazy voice. "Perhaps the best pick of London."

Sapphire grinned at Emerald. "See?" she said. "The best pick of London, that's us!"

Emerald smiled weakly. "You, perhaps."

"Yes, remarkably good views all round," said another one of the gentlemen.

One of them snorted. "Oh, I wouldn't say that! Why, there's a cripple just there with only one hand!"

Emerald watched as Sapphire's face immediately fell, all laughter gone, her eyes downcast, a flush tinged her cheeks.

*Oh, no. That was not to be permitted.*

"Excuse me," said Emerald, pulling away from her sister and pushing her way into the gaggle of gentlemen, most of whom awkwardly took a step back in the face of her anger. "I believe you just made a disparaging comment about my sister, and I have come for your apology."

"Ems, it doesn't matter—"

"I only said," said one of the young men, a ridiculous crimson cravat now starting to match his nose and cheeks, "that she—"

"I heard what you said, I have no wish to hear it again," Emerald snapped. Blood roared through her veins, she could practically hear her pulse, and though terror stirred in her chest, it was accompanied by something else. Rage. "And as I said, I am here for your apology."

Sapphire tugged her arm, clearly desperate to get away from the awful men, but Emerald stood her ground. She may not like people, but usually, that was no fault on them. That was her own shyness, her hatred of crowds.

*But people like this? Oh, they deserved to be hated.*

"I-I do apologize," stammered the idiot before her. "I did not mean—one cannot help but notice—"

"I will thank you for your apology, though 'tis meanly meant, and will give you some advice," bit back Emerald, hating how those around them were looking over. *Lord, was that person pointing?* "I advise you, most strongly, to keep your idiotic opinions to yourself if you are ever so unfortunate to be invited out into Society again. My sister's godmother, Lady Romeril, does not take kindly to such words."

The man's face, previously scarlet, immediately drained of color. "Lady Romeril?"

Several of his friends had disappeared, and Emerald saw with some satisfaction that he looked quite desperate to leave with them. "Lady Romeril," she repeated sweetly. "In fact, she should be here any moment. I think I would leave if I were you."

Stumbling backward and stammering words she could not

make out, the man rushed out of the ballroom, and Emerald watched with some satisfaction.

Then her shoulders sagged. All the power and determination she had felt in that moment, the need to protect her sister from such rogues, dissipated, leaving only fear.

"Thank you," Sapphire said in a small voice.

Emerald tried to take a breath. "Think nothing of it."

"But everyone is watching," her sister said quietly. "And you hate attention."

Taking a breath was proving to be rather difficult, especially now Sapphire had pointed out how much notice they had attracted thanks to her outburst. A few people were still pointing, and there was laughter in one quarter that Emerald had a horrible feeling was something to do with her.

She glanced at her sister. Sapphire had folded her arms, her stub—as she called it—carefully tucked into a glove she had modified herself, now hidden under her arm.

Emerald's heart twisted painfully. They never saw Sapphy as different—irritating, too quick to speak, and utterly embarrassing in company—but never different.

But their mother had been right. Coral had been right. The world would look at her differently.

"I hate attention," she said quietly, "but that does not mean I am going to leave you to the wolves."

Sapphire nodded without saying anything, and the two sisters stood for a moment in silence. Emerald hoped her cheeks did not look as red as they felt. It was one thing to speak out for her sister, but it was quite another to look as though she had run down the length of the ballroom.

"Perhaps it would be best if we went home," Emerald said, inspiration striking. "We could take the carriage and—"

"What did that rogue say to you?"

"Get back!" Emerald snapped, whirling round to glare at the man who'd just sneered.

Except he wasn't sneering. He wasn't one of the gentlemen

who had been standing with that scoundrel either; he was older, more mature.

*Far more handsome.*

Emerald pushed aside the thought immediately. She was not here to find connections, friends, or a husband. She was here because of an agreement, a compromise, and she had just snapped at a perfectly innocent man who appeared to be concerned for her.

*With me,* she thought wryly. Probably thought she was a harlot here to make trouble.

"I merely wished to ascertain whether you were quite well, after such a hideous encounter," said the gentleman, an eyebrow raised. "I know Orrinshire well, I can have the whole pack of them thrown out."

"Will you duel him?" asked Sapphire eagerly, stepping forward.

"There will be no need for that," Emerald said hastily, putting out an arm to prevent Sapphire from intruding too heavily on the man's space.

*Really, she was a liability!*

"I am afraid I am not a dueling sort of man," he said with a wry smile. "Besides, I believe your friend…sister?"

"Sister," said Sapphire before Emerald could remind her of the impropriety of speaking with a gentleman to whom they were not introduced. "I'm Sapphire, and this is Emerald. De Petras. Lord, I suppose I should have started with that."

"There you are!"

Emerald looked round with relief to see a familiar face. The arrival of James Gresley, Earl of Maltravers and long-term friend to the de Petras family, was a great comfort.

"Ah, Maltravers, wonderful," she said vaguely. "Sapphire, go dance with Maltravers."

"Dance with James?" Sapphire laughed as she scrunched up her nose. "But James doesn't want to dance with me, do you?"

Emerald smiled as a light flush covered their friend's cheeks.

"Oh, it wouldn't be the end of the world," said Maltravers with a dry laugh. "Come on, they're making up a set."

"I hope not a country dance, I can't stand them!"

Sapphire continued to chatter as she walked off arm in arm with Maltravers, and Emerald let out a low sigh. At least with him, she could be certain Sapphire wouldn't get into too much mischief. They had known Maltravers for years, ever since they were children. He was wise to Sapphire's mischief—and more importantly, would roundly defend her if needed.

"That leaves you with me, Miss de Petras."

Emerald turned to look up at the man to whom she had been so rude. "I suppose it does."

He waited patiently for her to continue, but Emerald was not entirely sure what he expected her to say. She did not even know his name, for goodness' sake, and there was no polite way for a lady to ask a gentleman's name.

"You look very pretty."

Emerald dropped her gaze immediately to her hands. *He was trying to flirt with her!* At least, he had paid her a compliment that was neither true nor impressive. What on earth was the man trying to do?

"My name is Swindmore," he said, and Emerald was forced to meet his eyes.

"Miss de Petras," Emerald mumbled, despite the fact he already knew her name.

She bobbed a curtsey, turned away, and started walking along the edge of the dancefloor. Anything to escape him, anything for a bit of peace. She had only been at the Orrinshire ball for twenty minutes, and in that time—

"I have heard of your family, of course," said Mr. Swindmore, walking alongside her. "Your mother is one of the most fashionable people in the *ton*. I see where you get it from."

Heat once again seared Emerald's cheeks as she increased her pace, rushing past a table where punch was being served and almost knocking over a gentleman coming the other direction.

But the trouble was, Mr. Swindmore was remarkably quick on his feet and, thanks to his height, had a longer pace.

Emerald halted, unable to continue any longer. "What do you want from me?"

She had not intended her words to be so direct, but there it was.

Mr. Swindmore's eyes widened. "I beg your pardon?"

"I have no interest in flirting, nor conversation, nor dancing, nor anything of the sort," said Emerald blandly, trying to meet his eyes and deciding that focusing on his jaw would be easier. At least, it would be if she had not just noticed how decidedly chiseled it was. "I do not even wish to be here at all, in truth, so I recommend you find another woman to—"

"What?" he interrupted with a smile. "Seduce?"

*Seduce! What a thing to say to a woman he has just met!*

"Goodness, you do intrigue me, Miss de Petras," said the rather inconvenient Mr. Swindmore. "Is there something wrong with me, that you desire to escape my presence so?"

"Not at all," Emerald said faintly. Oh, why would he not leave her alone?

A strange sort of hope that he would not think there was anything wrong with her flittered across her mind, but she pushed it aside.

She was not here to make a match. She had been perfectly clear with her mother, with the whole de Petras family. She did not wish to be married!

"You know what I think?"

Despite her instincts, Emerald looked up. Mr. Swindmore was grinning, a most charming smile, and her stomach lurched. No man that handsome had ever smiled at her. Had ever looked at her.

She shook her head, not trusting her voice.

"I think I am going to seduce you," said Mr. Swindmore happily.

Emerald's jaw dropped. "You cannot be serious."

"Why not?" he said with a laugh. "I find myself with nothing much else to do now the Season is coming to an end, and I may as well enjoy myself with a beautiful woman."

There was nothing she could do, nothing she could say to stop him from announcing such ridiculous things! Emerald's stomach churned, knowing beyond a shadow of a doubt that this was a disaster.

Oh, that she had never gained his attention in the first place!

"Absolutely not," she said firmly. "I do not wish to be married and have no desire at all to be seduced."

Mr. Swindmore's smile curled into a wicked grin. "Marvelous. I do so love a challenge."

# CHAPTER FOUR

*April 26, 1810*

"IT ABSOLUTELY CANNOT be that much," said Robert through gritted teeth.

He was not going to lose his temper. Probably. Though sorely pushed, though tempted at every moment to grasp the foolish man by his collar and drag him over that counter and make him see reason—

"I am afraid it is, my lord," said the haberdasher with lowered eyes.

Slowly, carefully, he took a deep breath. This was no time to allow his bitterness to surface—nor the place, either.

Robert turned to smile weakly at the gaggle of ladies behind him, examining ribbons, arguing over whether a certain shade of blue would bring out their eyes or just look ridiculous, then turned back to Mr. Rivers.

*It was not the man's fault,* he reminded himself. It was not his own fault either, but that did not make it the haberdasher's fault.

This was all *her* fault. Still, he had promised himself he would be free of her, and this was one of the last bills he had to pay off.

"I do apologize, Mr. Rivers, but I think you need to check your records again," said Robert as carefully as he could manage. "It is simply not possible!"

Two hundred pounds! When the invoice had arrived at his London townhouse, Robert had almost spat out his mouthful of tea when he saw the number at the bottom of the list.

The long list.

He had never spent that much on his apparel in his life! Probably. At the very least, not in one visit, which was apparently all it took for Isabelle to avail herself of the majority of the man's shop.

Robert glared about the place, taking in the bolts of fabric, the luxurious silks, the fur at one end, perfect for stoles. It was a wonder there was anything left in the place, after Isabelle.

But he absolutely refused to pay the entire thing, of that he was certain. She was no longer his wife, Robert reminded himself. He did not have to do this. She should be grateful, getting on bended knee and thanking him! Not that that was very likely…

A bead of sweat dribbled down the side of the haberdasher's head. "I am sorry, my lord, but at no point did I believe it inappropriate to give the marchioness—"

"Miss Ashby," interrupted Robert with a steely glare.

Why did his heart rail so much at the sound of marchioness? How was it possible that after just a year or two, he could already be so…so empty?

"Miss Ashby, yes, that is what I meant," said Mr. Rivers hastily. Another bead of sweat trickled down his forehead. "As I say, if I had known her credit was no good, I would never have dreamed of—"

"Yes, yes," said Robert, waving a hand. "I know. I know."

It had been the same story at the drapers. The drapers! To think the dratted woman had the audacity to send him the bill for the drapers for her new rooms. Robert had been forced to pay that one, too. If he was not careful, she would ruin him.

"And I must apologize to your lordship, it is most regrettable…"

The man's voice trailed off into the distance, and the fear in his voice caught Robert's attention. What on earth could the man be worried about now? Was not the worst over? Had not the inordinately long bill already been presented?

Hands slightly shaking, the haberdasher reached slowly under the desk and brought out another piece of paper.

Robert groaned. "Not more, please, I beg you."

"I-I truly believe this is the last," said Mr. Rivers with an awkward smile. "A last-minute order, she said…it arrived just after I had forwarded her first bill to you."

It was intolerable, but there it was. Robert could see no way around it, no opportunity to escape his responsibility. When Isabelle had racked up these bills, she had been his wife.

"I will admit, I am irritated about the whole endeavor," he said bad-tempered, bringing out his pocketbook and opening it up.

*Far emptier than it had been this morning.* Well, if that was the only way to cut the last ties with her…he had known that piece of paper at old Hamble's office was far too simple. He should have known there would be something to bite him at the end.

"I am sorry, your lordship," said the haberdasher.

Robert glanced at the man. Well, it wasn't his fault. He was a shopkeeper, and his job was to sell things. So, he had sold them.

Really, he ought to be commended for having been able to shift so much with just one customer.

One hundred gold buttons!

"There," he said, thrusting forward a sheaf of paper notes. "I believe that covers it all."

Mr. Rivers's eyes widened. Robert would not have been surprised if he had never seen so much money in his entire life, not all in one place. Not when that place was his hand.

"My lord," breathed the haberdasher.

"But that is the last bill I will receive from you on this account, do you hear me?" said Robert firmly. "No more. Absolutely no more."

He placed his pocketbook back inside his coat pocket, determined to quit this place at once and find some relief in a gaming hall somewhere—anywhere—but Robert was rather arrested when he turned around and clapped eyes on a woman at the back of the haberdashery, near the ribbons, with dark hair.

Dark hair he recognized.

*"I have no interest in flirting, nor conversation, nor dancing, nor anything of the sort. I do not even wish to be here at all, in truth, so I recommend you find another woman…"*

A slow smile crept across Robert's face. *Of course.* The woman from the ball. The one who had not made any sense to him, shy and nervous when she had first appeared, who had then firmly admonished that cad for something ill he had said about her sister.

*"I heard what you said, I have no wish to hear it again. And as I said, I am here for your apology."*

A ripple of interest meandered across his mind. She was fascinating. Even now, she pointedly ignored the rest of the world with no interest in it whatsoever. She looked at the ribbons closely, in silence.

So different from the other ladies in the shop, exclaiming loudly which colors were in this Season, and how they would absolutely have to throw out all their ribbons from last year.

*Emerald de Petras.*

The name surfaced without Robert having to seek it. She had been charming, a bit strange, and intriguing. Especially that little challenge she gave him. His mouth curled into a smile at the mere remembrance of it.

*"I do not wish to be married and have no desire at all to be seduced."*

*"Marvelous. I do so love a challenge."*

Well, it was not as though his heart was in any danger of being lost. Robert was not sure whether he still had a heart, in truth. Isabelle had stolen it quite away, and as far as he was concerned, she had not given it back.

Still. There was nothing wrong with a little diversion, a little seduction. Hiding away his heart was not necessary when such a wallflower was before him.

"Good afternoon, Miss de Petras."

Emerald dropped the two ribbons she had been examining, gave a small squeak, and turned to face him with blushing cheeks.

Robert grinned. It was good to see he was having an effect on a lady again. How long had it been? He had barely spoken to another woman since he had been married, and Isabelle had not spoken to him in almost nine months, only looking at him with contempt.

But Emerald de Petras did not look at him like that.

True, she looked at him more as though he were a wolf about to devour her...*not a bad idea*, thought Robert mischievously.

"S-Sir," she said quietly, picking up the fallen ribbons and refusing to meet his gaze.

"You would look remarkably pretty in a gown of that color," Robert said boldly, pointing at the blue ribbon in her left hand.

The flush on Emerald's cheeks, if possible, darkened.

My word, he had never seen a woman of this age stay such a wallflower. Was that not something that most ladies...well. *Got over? Grew out of?* Robert could not think of another phrase for it. Certainly, he did not see many misses of this age still stumble over their words, unable to look a gentleman in the eyes.

Robert looked closer. She was not a chit, that was certain, though she was not what Society would consider a spinster. A real woman.

Something lurched in his stomach—something that he heartily pushed away. No. He was not going to permit himself to be so easily fooled.

"I have no need of new gowns."

If Robert had not been paying careful attention, he would not have noticed nor heard the words that slipped from Emerald's mouth.

*Miss de Petras,* he thought firmly. Not Emerald. Far too intimate.

She had spoken softly, still not meeting his eyes, and Robert was taken with a desire to see those pretty pupils. A hazel sort of green, from memory. Not a color one saw often.

"I must say, it is pleasant indeed to have such an effect on a lady," he said quietly.

The hustle and bustle of the haberdashery continued around them, but his words finally sparked a response.

Emerald looked up, her hazel eyes flashing. "You do not have such an effect—I mean…I am shy around everyone. It's not just you."

Her gaze dropped to her hands clasped before her, and Robert's mouth fell open.

*Not have any—not just him?*

Why, the rudeness of the woman! Saying he had no more effect on her than anyone else…it was unconscionable.

*It may just well be true,* a rather irritatingly reasonable part of him whispered. Why, she was certainly a wallflower at the ball, and looked remarkably discomforted when she had entered on the arms of her sister and a woman who could only be their mother.

So, was it true? Was it possible it was not his…his good looks and charm, but rather the mere fact he was a gentleman that had her flushing so prettily?

Robert cleared his throat. "I refuse to believe it."

"You can believe it or not, that is your choice," came the quiet reply. "I do not mind."

*The cheek of this woman!* And yet not cheek—it was more delicate than that. The boldness! No, that was not right either…

It was a strange mixture of boldness and fear, a heady combination of rebellion and capitulation, and Robert had never encountered anything like it.

A flash of green eyes. Emerald had looked up and seen his astonishment. Was that a small smile on her lips?

Robert closed his mouth hurriedly and tried to search for the right way to respond in this absolutely ridiculous conversation.

"Ah, Miss de Petras," said Mr. Rivers, bustling over with a

pair of gloves. "There you are, a matching glove for the one you lost."

She took the gloves without saying a word, without lifting her eyes.

Apparently, this was expected. Mr. Rivers bowed, then returned to his counter.

Robert swallowed most uncomfortably. Ah. Well, his ego was always going to take a knock at some time. He had just never expected it to be so utterly destroyed by a wallflower.

"I see," he said quietly.

This time Emerald did not look away. "'Tis nothing personal, sir."

"No, I can see that," Robert said dryly.

"I-I meant—"

"I know what you meant," he cut in. "Well, you have certainly demonstrated it perfectly. My goodness, Miss de Petras. I wish I had believed you from the start."

Was that a wry smile? It had disappeared the moment he had seen it, and Robert found himself unusually intrigued by the woman before him. Had he taken a step forward? Was that why they seemed that much closer, the rest of the shop fading away into the background?

"My mother called me a contrary debutante recently," said Emerald softly, her voice hardly rising above a whisper. "A-And though I am no debutante, I am rather contrary."

*Rather contrary?* Robert's stomach lurched. Why, this woman could hardly be less contrary if she tried! This shy, nervous thing? She probably obeyed her parents to a fault, never spoke back, and never argued with anything anyone said.

Except she had, hadn't she?

*"I do not wish to be married and have no desire at all to be seduced."*

*"Marvelous. I do so love a challenge."*

Robert took a step closer and watched as Emerald shrank back into the rack of ribbons. "I greatly enjoyed the ball we attended. Did you?"

She shook her head, her gaze on him as though she could not remove it. "N-No."

"Is that because you did not dance?" persisted Robert, watching as her pupils dilated, her hands clutched together a little tighter.

No matter what she said, he was certain he had an effect on her. A strange effect, certainly.

Because she was not afraid of him. He could see that in her eyes; there was no fear. More…discomfort. This was not the sort of conversation she was accustomed to.

"Tell me, Emerald—"

"Miss de Petras." Her voice was firm, as though certain things could not be permitted.

He recalled how vehemently she had defended her sister. *Interesting.* A wallflower, then, with thorns underneath such pretty blossoms…

"I prefer Emerald," Robert said, allowing just a hint of charm to seep into his tone. "Emerald, like your eyes."

Emerald snorted, then raised her hands to her mouth with horror. "I-I mean—"

"I know exactly what you mean," he cut across her.

*Well.* This wallflower was far more interesting than he had thought. When he had first seen her at the ball, pretty but with absolutely no interest in being there, the woman had radiated indifference. He had thought her naught but entertainment for an evening.

Perhaps a night if he were lucky.

But Emerald de Petras was far more than that, wasn't she? Far bolder, underneath. Far more opinionated than she wanted to let on. Far more interesting.

"Tell me," Robert said, neglecting to choose a name for her this time, "at the next ball, will you dance with me?"

"I will never dance with you," came the gasped reply.

It was as though he had said something obscene, scandalous.

Her eyes, if possible, were even wider, and he noted the flush had descended from her cheeks and was now coloring her throat. Below her throat…

Robert jerked his head upward. He was in a public place—he was in a haberdashery, for goodness' sake! He could not be spotted staring at a woman's décolletage!

It was too late. Emerald had dropped her gaze, pulling her light pelisse around her more tightly, covering the front of her gown entirely.

Damn. Only now that he had lost her gaze did Robert realize how delicious she was.

"You will not dance with me?"

Emerald shook her head. "No, but you must not see this as a personal slight."

"I am learning nothing you say to me is personal, Miss de Petras."

She laughed—one that could be easily ignored, but he was becoming so quickly attuned to every noise she made, every movement, that he saw it immediately.

And then the merriment was gone.

Dear Lord, she was a challenge. This was not a woman who would soon fall into his arms as soon as she heard the title *marquess*. She was not impressed by riches, not that he had much, nor a good name, which he did.

No, she was far more interesting than that. *Damn.*

"You know, you are making yourself into more of a challenge with every passing moment," Robert breathed.

Emerald met his gaze. "Well, I am sorry to disappoint, but I am not a prize to be won."

He swallowed. *If only.*

"Besides, I will not be in Society much longer."

"You won't?" Why did his heart splutter at the very idea? Society, without Emerald? It was not a thought to be entertained, let alone considered.

Emerald nodded. "I have agreed with my mother to attend

ten balls at the end of this Season, then no more. The ball where you met me was the first."

"That leaves me nine balls to convince you to dance with me," said Robert.

He spoke lightly, but his heart was not. Ten balls. Ten balls, and then she would retreat from Society forever? This was no wallflower, but some other breed entirely. He had never known a woman so beautiful, so elegantly charming—shy, yes, but that did not detract from her charms—to be so unwilling to be a part of Society.

What was Emerald de Petras's story?

"As I said," Emerald spoke in a low voice, "I will not dance with you."

"And you don't want to be married?"

The words had slipped from Robert's lips before he could stop them, his heart overwhelmed with the sight of Emerald, the thought of only having nine more opportunities to see those eyes, that lithe figure…

*Marriage.* He was hardly the person to be speaking of such an estate. It was not as though he had a particularly impressive record.

The word had caused, it seemed, just as strong a reaction in Emerald as it had within him. Her cheeks darkened slightly, but she did not lower her gaze. In fact, her chin jutted out slightly as though she had had this argument before.

"I will never be married," she said.

Robert stared. This woman…he could not understand her, and it was quite clear that she had no wish to be understood. It was intriguing. It was confusing.

It was fast making her the most interesting person he had ever met.

"You are staring at me."

Robert chuckled darkly. "I am indeed."

Emerald swallowed. "W-Well I—I wish you wouldn't."

"There is no law against looking at a beautiful woman."

She half-turned away from him, as though his words over-whelmed her—as though he overwhelmed her. But Robert knew better than to think so highly of himself. This was a woman who hated Society, it appeared, hated balls, hated company…enough to sacrifice her hopes for matrimony?

Perhaps she had been jilted. Perhaps she had been seduced, bedded, and abandoned.

Whatever it was, she appeared to be just as bitter as he was, just as jaded with the ideas of love and matrimony and the *ton*.

Perhaps, just perhaps, she could be convinced into an arrangement…

"I must be going."

Robert started. "Going? Going where?"

Emerald smiled nervously and stepped away from him. Every inch that now separated them seemed a gulf between them. Robert somehow stuck to the floor, unable to follow her.

"I cannot be seen here, conversing with a gentleman," she said lightly. "What will people think?"

# CHAPTER FIVE

*April 28, 1810*

T HE SECOND BALL.

It turned out that despite telling herself not to be nervous with each and every step that she took from the carriage to the rather large townhouse outside which they had been deposited, Emerald was not able to actually prevent her heart from fluttering.

*It's just a ball.*

Just an opportunity for people to tell her over and over again how fortunate her sister was, and why had she not managed to win a duke when she was still on the shelf…

Emerald swallowed as they stepped into the hallway, gave their wraps to the footmen, and stepped forward into the ballroom.

Just a ball.

At the very least, she should be celebrating, Emerald tried to tell herself as she accepted a glass of punch from a silver platter offered to her. The liquid quivered in the glass as her hand shook. She took a gulp, hoping that would make it less obvious.

The remaining liquid quivered just as much.

"Do not fret so," murmured her mother under her breath.

Emerald glanced at Opal and wished to goodness she had

inherited a little of the de Petras boldness. Coral had it, Micah had it. Sapphire arguably had too much of it.

But she…she had none of it. None at all.

*"That leaves me nine balls to convince you to dance with me."*

*"As I said, I will not dance with you."*

Her hand shook so violently, punch dribbled down the side of her glass onto her hand.

"Emerald!"

"Sorry," she said hastily, hating how swiftly her mother drew attention to the smallest of indiscretions. "It's only on my hand."

"Oh, you'll be all sticky now and goodness knows how we will clean it off," muttered Opal, glancing around for a footman. "Really, Emerald—"

"What has she done now?" sighed Micah.

Emerald shot a look of desperation to her brother, but he did not seem in the mood to help. Not that he ever was. No, Micah was looking about the place quite imperiously, as though he had something far better to do than attend a ball hosted by the Braedons.

"Spilt her drink," murmured Opal.

"It's just a splash," said Sapphire, taking the glass from Emerald and pouring the liquid down her throat in one gulp. "There you go, all gone."

Emerald could not help but smile as their mother stared, outraged, at the way her youngest had put away such a quantity of punch.

"Sapphire de Petras!"

"Oh, don't make a fuss," said Sapphire good-naturedly. She handed the empty glass to a passing footman and shot a grin at her sister. "Don't have too much fun will you, Ems?"

With that, she wandered off and struck up a conversation with a pair of ladies. A pair of ladies that, to Emerald's knowledge, her sister had never met before.

*How did she do it?* Was there something magical in the air when Sapphy had been born, for it was not a skill one could learn.

If so, Emerald would have mastered it long ago.

"You should not make such a spectacle of yourself, Emerald," chastised her mother.

Emerald gaped. "M-Me? Sapphy is out there introducing herself to goodness knows who, and Micah—"

"Go on, what am I doing wrong?" snapped her brother.

Heat seared her cheeks. She was merely going to say that her brother hardly ever attended balls anymore and appeared to have as little interest in matrimony as she did, but her words were stolen from her throat by his glare.

"I-I…I did not…"

"Oh, hush with you, Micah," said their mother ill-temperedly as the music started and a few couples gravitated together to form a line. "I suppose I shall not have the pleasure of seeing all three of my unwed children standing up to dance this evening?"

*"As I said, I will not dance with you."*

Emerald swallowed and shook her head. She was not going to dance. She'd been perfectly clear with Robert—with *him* about it. Besides, he was not here. Not that she'd looked.

Oh, it was so foolish of her. She could not have made a worse impression the first time they had met—the words she had shouted at those gentlemen, absolutely outrageous!—and the second time, she had barely been able to string two coherent words together.

No, it was a blessing he was not here.

"What is this, ball number two?" said Micah with a heavy sigh.

Emerald nodded, still not trusting her voice. Yes, her second ball. Excruciating though it was, it did mean she was twenty percent of the way through. One in five. Anything she could think to convince herself that this terrible nightmare would soon be over.

This contrary debutante, as her family was now never ceasing to call her, could then retire at home, happier than she ever had been in company.

Micah sniffed. "I hope you know it's all your fault that I am here, Ems."

Emerald stared at her brother as he looked out at the guests as though searching for someone. "Me?"

"That is not quite true though, is it?" said Opal pointedly. "I hope Lady Romeril is here, I am in anticipation of hearing whether—"

"Mother does not believe you two girls can behave yourselves," said Micah with a wicked grin.

Emerald gaped, then closed her mouth hurriedly. Unladylike behavior was not to be tolerated. "Behave ourselves?"

Opal sighed. "That's not what I said, Micah, I wish you would not turn my words—"

"After that first ball you went to, when you attacked those young men—"

"I attacked no one!" Emerald tried to keep her voice low, calm, but it was a challenge.

*That was not what had happened at all!* And if Micah had bothered to ask her about it, he would have known precisely why she had said what she did.

Rage bubbled up inside Emerald at the mere memory of what those blaggards had said about Sapphire. They all protected her, always.

A loud giggle echoed across the ballroom. The three de Petrases looked over and saw Sapphire surrounded by a gaggle of gentlemen, tipping her head back and laughing as they fawned over her.

A wry smile crept across Emerald's face. Not that Sapphire often needed protecting.

"My point is, I could have been somewhere far more interesting tonight if it wasn't for you," said Micah heavily. "Lord, there isn't a half-decent woman about the place."

"Micah!"

"Mother," he said sarcastically.

Emerald swallowed. They were beginning to attract attention, and not the sort their mother would wish. Was that an older gentleman pointing at them, as he muttered something in the ear of his friend?

"You will never find a wife if you do not smile more," said Opal, looking around carefully.

A flicker of tension arched across Emerald's shoulders. If only they could just leave…just fade into the background. No one would miss them, surely? At least, no one would miss her. Perhaps if her mother became distracted by Micah, she could just slip away and—

"I have plenty of mistresses, Mama, I am not looking for a wife."

"Hush," Emerald breathed, unable to take it anymore.

Opal's cheeks were flushed now. Emerald could not recall having seen her mother look quite this unsettled, but then, it was rare that Micah was so foolish as to say such things at all, let alone in public.

It was not as though the de Petras family were not quite aware that Micah had…lady friends, as their father had so delicately put it.

The money had to go somewhere.

But Micah had usually been relatively discreet. *Relatively,* Emerald thought with a wry laugh. She had once seen a woman slip out of their home at a very early hour, far earlier than could be acceptable, but she had never said anything to her brother. What would she say?

"People are watching," Emerald breathed, wishing she could speak even lower but unsure whether her mother and brother would actually hear her.

Micah had the good grace to look a little embarrassed. "I did not mean…darn it all, Mama, you know I am not interested in—"

"Let us just stand here for a moment and say nothing," said Opal sternly.

Emerald watched as Opal picked a spot in the middle distance to stare at, as Micah pursed his lips as though he was a child.

She sighed and settled into the silence. At least that was something she was good at. Staying silent and attempting not to draw any attention to herself. Easy.

"—never seen them all together, but then there are so many of them—"

"I heard the mother gained her fortune through stealth or some criminal activity—"

"No!"

"I declare, the de Petrases have far more money than I would expect for a woman—"

"—definitely something dodgy about her—"

The speakers passed them by, seemingly unaware the people they were gossiping about had been standing right before them.

Emerald's cheeks burned so hotly, she felt branded. Her mind swirled with panic, breath caught in her throat, her fingers tingling as they clasped together before her.

Such gossip. Such scandalous suppositions!

*"I heard the mother gained her fortune through stealth or some criminal activity—"*

Emerald glanced at her mother. Unusually for Opal de Petras, typically an unflappable woman—something she had always admired—Emerald saw discomfort in her eyes.

Emerald could not believe it. There could not be any truth in those words, could there?

Their family was unusual, to be sure. Emerald had hated it when she had first entered Society, whippersnapper gentlemen inquiring just how it worked, with her mother as the head of the family rather than her father, and had become tired of constantly explaining—*justifying, Coral had called it*—the way the daughters would keep their names after marriage.

But stealth, illegal activity…something criminal? Surely not!

"It's not true," muttered Micah.

Emerald looked up to see her brother looking fiercely at her, as though desperate to convince her of his words.

"It is not true," he emphasized again in a low voice. "You

must not give any credit to it, Ems. It's just nasty gossip, you know what Society is like."

"I-I do indeed," Emerald managed to say, trying desperately to smile. "Why do you think I wish to stay out of it as much as possible?"

Micah breathed a laugh, then glanced at their mother. Emerald looked at her, too. Opal still looked flushed, discomforted, as though she had been personally slighted.

Which she had, of course. If such rumors could be overheard at a ball, they were certainly being discussed in the gaming hells and drawing rooms of the *ton*, Emerald knew.

They would have to tell Coral. As their mother's heir—

"Ah, Mrs. de Petras," said a smooth, confident voice. "I had hoped I would have the chance to be introduced to you."

Emerald froze. No. She must be dreaming. She certainly had to be imagining that sultry voice indelibly marked on her mind after that embarrassing encounter at the haberdashery…

She turned slowly on the spot and saw Robert grinning—not just at her, but her family.

"Oh, and you're here, too, Miss de Petras," he said lightly. "How delightful."

"It is not delightful!" The words had slipped out before she could stop them, and Emerald fought the instinct to bring her hands to her mouth.

She was not going to permit herself to be overwhelmed by him. She was not!

But her wishes did not seem to matter. Robert was looking at her—Mr.…oh blast, she could not recall his name. Whoever he was, then, was looking at her as though she was being remarkably amusing.

Now, if only she could separate him from—

"Good evening, sir," said Opal, her winning smile reappearing as she looked between the stranger and her daughter. "Always a pleasure to meet such a handsome gentleman."

She offered her hand, and Robert took it, kissing it and then shooting a wink at Emerald.

Emerald blanched. She had to escape this nightmare, for now, he had done such a thing, such a forward and teasing thing, there was no possibility her mother would not get…what was it Coral had said once?

*Ideas.*

Opal beamed at her daughter, and Emerald groaned. She had got ideas.

"Oh, I did not know you were acquainted with my daughter, how delightful," Opal almost purred. "You know, I have said to Emerald several times, there are just so many young men courting her, it is hard to keep track…"

She fluttered on for what felt to Emerald like several minutes, each one of them awful. If only the Braedons' ballroom could swallow her, cracking open and taking her down into the depths. It had to be better than this, did it not?

"—and now here you are," finished her mother prettily. "I suppose you came over here to ask my daughter to dance."

"Mama!"

"Of course, I did," said Robert with a bow of his head.

Emerald glared, and he had the good manners to look a little rueful. He knew precisely what she had said merely days ago, did he not? Well, he was just going to have to become accustomed to disappointment.

"As I said before," Emerald said sweetly, "I will not dance with you."

"You will!" hissed her mother.

"Absolutely not."

Emerald glanced at her brother, but it appeared Micah had lost interest in the conversation. He was staring across the room intently, and she could not help but look also.

Her cheeks pinked. Miss Tilbury, known harlot, was chatting in a lively manner with a pair of gentlemen. Surely her brother had not—

"You—you truly will not dance with me?"

Emerald jerked her head back to the gentleman before her and was surprised to see a look of astonishment on Robert's face. Had she not been perfectly clear?

"I am a woman of my word, sir," she said stiffly. "When I told you I would not dance with you, I meant it."

"You told him what?"

"And as I also said," Emerald continued, forcefully ignoring her mother and wishing this whole ridiculous conversation could be over with, "I have no interest in—in being a challenge, and so good day to you sir."

It was all she could do not to retreat, but a small part of her was determined not to give him that satisfaction. Besides, the ballroom was filling up fast. There would soon be few places she could hide, more's the pity.

Emerald glanced at the handsome gentleman before her, whose mouth was now open.

"Oh, just leave her, man," said Micah irritably. "Don't waste your time."

Without another word, he sauntered off in the direction of Miss Tilbury, leaving Emerald to gather her breath and try not to be too hurt by her brother's words.

Well, she had known his opinion of her, had she not? That she was not worth worrying about, that no gentleman should bother speaking to her. It was hardly a secret, though Micah had never spelled it out in quite those words before.

Her cheeks must be scarlet; she was certain they were. If only she had never made this bargain with her mother!

"Micah!" Opal rushed after her son, leaving Emerald quite alone with her unwanted suitor.

Emerald tried not to think about it. Tried not to think that she was standing here with a gentleman, alone. At least, as alone as one could become in a ballroom.

"Your brother, at least I assume that is your brother, does not seem to think very much of you."

She looked up. Robert had a strange look on his face, close to anger. He had, at the very least, not supposed Micah was one of those "countless suitors" her mother had so foolishly spoken of.

Emerald tried to smile, though it was difficult. "He does not think much of any of us."

She should not have said such a thing—she felt it the moment the words had slipped past her lips—but there was nothing she could do about it. Airing family dirty laundry at a ball was not right—an error she would have expected from Sapphire!

"B-But I suppose all families have their quarrels, do they not?" Emerald tried to say as calmly as she could. Yes, small talk, light conversation. Surely she could manage that? "Do you find the same in your family?"

Robert shrugged. A footman pushed past him, forcing him to take a step forward, and most unfortunately Emerald could feel a woman standing behind her, preventing her retreat.

He was close now. Robert. Whatever his name was.

"I am afraid there is not much to tell when it comes to my family," he said with a nonchalant grin. "No brothers and sisters, a mother who died young, and a father who died about five years ago."

"You are alone then," Emerald said.

*Alone.* True, it was something she craved, solitude, but there was something different about looking for solitude in a big family and having it forced upon you by the lack of one.

For the first time since their acquaintance, Emerald looked at him with compassion.

"Alone?" Robert laughed. "No, I would not say that. The estate has always kept me busy, until recently…I mean, servants keep one entertained. And thanks to the title—"

"The title?"

Emerald had not intended to interrupt. *Title?* She could not recall a title…though perhaps that was why she was struggling to place the gentleman's full name. Had it been simply too long for her to take in?

She smiled weakly as the music ended and those around them

gently applauded both dancers and musicians. "You will have to excuse me, I am not very good with names."

"But excellent with faces."

Emerald smiled, despite herself. "How did you know that?"

"I would imagine you have had to be one if you could not be the other," Robert said with a laugh. "Yes, the title. Robert Ainsworth, Marquess of Swindmore. I shall have to hope I have made a better impression this time."

Emerald swallowed. He was certainly far less…well, odious was a hard word, and she did not mean it. She had felt so defensive when she had first met him, so astonished to see him the second time…but this time she was more aware of him.

Aware of all of him. His height, the broadness of his shoulders, the way his eyes glittered when he looked at her. The way his looming height seemed to…invite something. Something she did not understand. Something she could not explain, but perhaps did not need to.

"Oh," Emerald said helplessly. "Well. My lord."

Robert gave her a wolfish grin. "So, will you dance with a marquess?"

She flushed. "No."

"No?"

Emerald swallowed. There was nothing keeping her here. She had attended her second ball and had stayed at least half an hour. That was more than she had managed last time. She was certain her mother would not complain.

"You must excuse me, my lord," she said, turning away from the handsome man who would definitely be intruding on her dreams that evening.

"Emerald? Miss de Petras!"

Emerald pushed through the crowd and managed to make the street, the chilly night air refreshing in her lungs.

That was close. If she had lingered much longer, she may have done the unthinkable.

She may have agreed to dance with him.

# CHAPTER SIX

*May 1, 1810*

*T**HE THIRD BALL.**
He was being an absolute fool, and the worst of it was,
he knew it.

Robert pulled awkwardly at his cravat, which had been tied
far too tight, and tried not to think about the fact that Isabelle
could appear at any moment.

*Surely not.* Surely after their divorce—something so scandalous, he had been forced to pay all the newspapers extortionate
money just to keep their names out of them—she would leave
London. Leave Society.

After all, she'd taken a not-insignificant amount of his fortune
with her. She could happily set up home somewhere pleasant—
Brighton, perhaps—and leave him alone.

Robert swallowed as a gaggle of ladies, all fans and feathers,
strode by him.

None of them were Isabelle.

It had been a mistake to come here. A mistake driven by
pride, and arrogance, and a determination to see Miss Emerald de
Petras eat her words.

*"As I said, I will not dance with you."*

Robert strode into a small room where ladies were seated,

chattering away, and scoured the place for women with dark hair and green eyes.

She was not here. Something within him crackled with the lack of her, his very skin aching for a touch.

He turned abruptly and left the room.

He was a fool. Robert had hoped the de Petras family would be here.

How was it possible that mere days had passed and he had not seen her?

He had intended only to seduce Emerald, and now he knew she had a family around who would certainly defend her honor, he should not even think of her. He should leave with no intention of seeking out Miss Emerald de Petras again. That would only lead to—

Robert stopped in his tracks. There she was. Emerald.

Just as he had thought her name, she had appeared before him. Well, on the other side of the ballroom, but there, in his line of vision. As though he had called her into being, as though his yearning for her—

*No, not yearning.* Robert swallowed, desperately trying to calm his breathing.

He must not permit himself to get overtaken by her. He had escaped the clutches of one woman so recently, he would not allow himself to sink into the embraces of another.

A wry smile crept across his face. As though Emerald would take him in her arms.

No, she had so far resisted every element of his attempted charm, though admittedly he had not truly tried. Not as he would do tonight.

A woman appeared at Emerald's side, comforting her. Robert could see the rigidity in her face, the fear, the tension that being in such a place clearly inspired.

*"I have agreed with my mother to attend ten balls at the end of this Season, then no more."*

Robert had been unable to stop thinking about it. This compromise of hers. Ten balls, each designed, it could not be more clear, by Mrs. de Petras to marry off her daughter.

Yes, there she was. The matriarch of the family stood by her two daughters, a mother hen clearly desperate to keep them safe from rogues, yet at the same time, if she was anything like the countless mothers Robert had met, marry them off.

Well, he was not about to allow himself to be caught, not again.

Matrimony was the swiftest way to get caught by a woman seeking nothing more than her own comfort, and he would not risk it again.

Still. It could not hurt to talk to them.

Against his better judgment, against all that he knew was right and sensible, Robert found himself drifting across the room toward the de Petras family.

The mother had wandered off, leaving the two daughters together. *All the better*, he thought with a smile. All the easier to get Emerald on her own, pull her into an alcove, and—

He was not going to get his heart entangled again. A man approached the sisters. He was welcomed eagerly, smiles on both their faces, and a rush of irritable jealousy washed through Robert until the man turned and he saw it was the same who had danced with the sister before.

Robert's hackles lowered, though he was a fool to allow himself to get so het up in the first place. This man was no competition for Emerald's heart—not that he was.

*Oh, blast.*

The gentleman said something that made the younger sis- ter—*Sapphire, was it?*—laugh, and once again that twist of irritation speared through Robert's chest. If only he could make the elder smile.

He caught Emerald's eye and saw her flush with what he must assume was pleasure to see him.

"Miss de Petras," Robert said, bowing before the two women. "Hullo—"

"I am not going to dance with you," said Emerald immediately, over her sister.

Robert blinked. How did she do it? Put him right back in his place as though he were not a marquess, hardly even a gentleman!

For a woman who protested she had no interest in balls, matrimony, Society, gossip, or gentlemen, she had a sharp tongue on her.

"Emerald! How can you say such a thing and to such a handsome gentleman, too!"

"Sapphire!"

"Really, Sapphy, you cannot say such things in public," said the gentleman with an awkward laugh.

Robert inclined his head to the gentleman and made a note to inquire as to his name later. He was evidently not a threat—not that he was seeking Emerald's hand.

*Oh, this was getting complicated.*

Still, he was evidently trusted by the family. Indeed, the younger looked at him with a rather shining adoration that, if Robert had been in the young man's shoes, would certainly have gone to his head.

"I can say whatever I want, as long as no one important hears me say it," Sapphire de Petras said haughtily, and then with a grin, "not that I mean any disparagement to you, sir."

Robert smiled weakly. *This one was a livewire and no mistake.* It was strange, for he could easily see how gentlemen would be taken by the younger Miss de Petras. And if he was not very much mistaken, the gentleman beside them already was. But somehow, all her brightness, boldness, and brashness did not compare to the simple and elegant beauty beside her.

His throat ached and his stomach lurched. Robert tried not to think of her. Emerald, just standing there gracefully, as though she was not being slowly mortified by her sister.

"I am, indeed, no one important," said Robert with a half-smile, attempting as best he could not to stare at Emerald. He would not be so easily taken in. Would he? "Indeed, I am so unimportant that despite asking three times before this very night, your sister will not dance with me."

"Emerald! Not dance with such a nice gentleman?" Sapphire raised an eyebrow and nudged her sister as though chastising her for her poor taste. "And to think, I would have given up after the second time. Truly, sir, you have asked three times?"

"Last time, she was most unaccountably rude," Robert said wryly.

"I was not!"

Ah—there she was. He had managed to force Emerald to speak, though she looked mightily unhappy about it. There was a brightness about her eyes.

Desires Robert had pushed aside for many months now rose up, unbidden, yet he knew precisely what they were.

"I suppose rude is perhaps a little strong," he said aloud. "But I will take it all back if you agree to dance with me."

If he had been bolder—if there had not been another gentleman standing beside him—Robert may have reached out and taken her hand. Surely the sensation of her hand in his, gloves or no, would have been enough to sway her.

But Robert had to admit to himself that he was...well. Rather running out of ideas.

Isabelle had not been this difficult.

Hindsight was a wonderful thing, naturally, but it was only now that he was starting to wonder whether his ease at bedding then wedding the woman may have had something to do with his fortune and her lack of one.

"I said I will not dance with you," said Emerald stiffly.

He would never be so uncouth as to force a woman, but her heart was not in her refusal. He could spot the signs: the flicker of intrigue, the way she had shifted in the group to be closer to him. The way she had not walked away. The smile teasing the edges of her lips.

Robert swallowed. She wanted to dance with him, craved to

give into the temptation, but she had made her bed, and now she had to lie in it.

Oh, God, the idea of Emerald de Petras in bed with him…

Forcing aside the thoughts that were not helping him in the slightest, Robert shrugged dramatically and sighed as though he had been denied life itself.

"You see, Miss Sapphire? How is a man to endure against such determination?"

"It is not personal, as I said before," said Emerald, her cheeks flushed.

Why was it that since that awful signing of divorce papers just weeks ago, no one had sparked any sort of joy but this woman?

"You say not to take it personally, and it is true that I have seen you stand up with no other gentleman," he conceded. "But I cannot help but wish that you would make it personal."

Emerald frowned. "I do not underst—"

"I wish you *would* dance with me," intercut Robert. Was this a normal flirtation? If so, why did he feel so strange? "Make me special, Miss de Petras. Make it personal. Make me the object of envy of every man in the place."

His voice had, for some reason, lowered. Perhaps that was why he had stepped closer to her—Robert could think of no other reason.

Her eyes had not left his, and something sparked between them Robert had not expected. Desire, heat, and longing all rushed through him in a moment, and then it was gone.

Someone cleared their throat.

Blinking, Robert saw the gentleman was looking rather sharply at him. *Ah.* Yes, well, that was a rather scandalous thing to suggest to a woman. In public. With her sister and a gentleman beside them.

He would not take the words back. Not after seeing their effect on Emerald.

Sapphire grinned. "You could always dance with me."

"No!"

It was not Emerald who had spoken, much to Robert's surprise, but the gentleman by Sapphire's side. As their eyes met, the young man flushed a dark crimson.

"I just…if you wished to dance, Sapphy, all you had to do was ask me."

"Oh, I've danced with you a thousand times, James," said Sapphire. "Come on, sir, I believe it's time I danced with a stranger."

Robert glanced for a moment at Emerald. He was not usually one to come between sisters, especially not those so different as these before him.

The older refined, quiet, seemingly terrified of crowds, and absolutely beautiful.

The younger just as pretty, but in an untidy way, hair loose with a mischievous grin.

But desperate times called for desperate measures. Emerald had made it perfectly clear she had no intention of dancing, and until Robert showed her what she was missing, there was no possibility of him enticing her into something so scandalous as dancing at a private ball.

Sapphire offered out her arm. There was no hand on it.

Robert blinked. He had almost forgotten, in the rush of their conversation, what had drawn his attention to Emerald in the first place—her insolent defense of her sister after some ruffians spoke ill of her.

And this was why.

Pushing past his moment of hesitation, Robert took the end of her wrist just as he would have taken any lady's hand and beamed at her sister.

"You will have to excuse me, Miss de Petras," he said with a grin. "I know you greatly wished to dance with me, but I can listen to your pleading no longer. I am now otherwise engaged."

"I never said—"

Robert turned and led Sapphire toward the dancers.

She grinned. "You passed the test, by the way."

*Test?* Goodness gracious, he could hardly keep up with this family. What with the brother who spoke disparagingly of one sister, that same sister defending a second when anyone spoke disparagingly of her—

"My stub," said Sapphire succinctly as they reached the set and Robert released her.

His eyes were pulled, despite his better judgement, toward the wrist with no hand.

"What…ahem. What about it?" he managed.

Well, it was not as though he had never seen anyone who was different. Plenty of men had returned from wars with no arms at all, he reasoned, as he stepped forward in time with the music. Some were born blind, others deaf.

Sapphire smiled, though without the bold grin he had come to expect. "That's just it. You did not mind it."

Was that all? Robert shrugged as they stepped to the left as the dance dictated. "I learned a long time ago that looks can be deceiving, in all directions. 'Tis best to ignore them."

"Except when you are looking at my sister," said Sapphire archly.

Robert almost tripped over his feet. When he righted himself, heart thumping, hoping to goodness Emerald hadn't noticed his clumsiness, it was to see Sapphire stifling giggles.

"I am sorry, sir—sorry, what is your name?"

"Robert Ainsworth, Marquess of Swindmore," was all Robert could manage.

"Lord, a marquess! Would that make my sister a marchioness, then?"

Was he so obvious? Was it clear to the world that he had an inkling of delight in Emerald de Petras? For goodness' sake, he did not even know it until her sister said it!

But he could not deny it, to her nor himself. His heart longed for her in a way that was utterly different from anything he had experienced with Isabelle.

That decision had been made by a very different part of his

body…

"Who is the gentleman accompanying you?" Robert said aloud.

The sooner they were able to get away from this topic of conversation, the better. Besides, the dance had turned him around and now he could see Emerald standing with the gentleman in question, as easily as if they were siblings.

Another flicker of jealousy crept around his heart. Who was he, this man who stood with such confidence by the de Petras sisters?

Sapphire followed his gaze, then snorted. "Oh, that's just James. Maltravers—sorry, the Earl of Maltravers. I've known him my whole life, you'll have to forgive my impertinence."

Robert would not have called it impertinence. It was rather lovely, actually. Whether Sapphire knew the man's designs on her, he would have to guess not…

"And he and your sister—I mean—"

"Just come out and say it, man, it's far easier that way," said Sapphire as she stepped forward, offering her hand and—what was it she had called it? Her stub?

Robert took both without hesitation. "You are far too observant for your own good, Miss Sapphire."

"That's what they tell me," she shot back. "But it doesn't take someone like me to see that you are interested in my sister. Aren't you?"

He did not reply immediately. He was too distracted by a pair of green eyes watching him meander down the set. Green eyes that flashed with—was that jealousy? Or was that only his heart speaking, a heart desperate for her to be envious of her sister?

"You are interested in Ems, aren't you?"

Robert swallowed. They had reached the end of the set, and now had nothing to do for a few bars of music. That led him, rather, unfortunately, to his own thoughts.

Thoughts about Emerald.

Though he was dancing with one woman, he could not help

but think about Emerald de Petras. The way she teased him with that look, that dancing smile that never quite seemed to settle. The cleverness of her eyes, the way she had defended her sister so resolutely.

There was something very interesting about Emerald, something no other man had seemingly bothered to discover.

"Not in the slightest," he lied.

Sapphire snorted again. "Do not bother lying to me, your lordship, it's as plain as the nose on your face. Emerald knows it."

Robert snapped his gaze away from the beautiful woman in question to the sharp one before him. "She does?"

"Why do you care?" Sapphire said, arching an eyebrow. "You told me you had no interest in her."

*Well, you couldn't argue with logic like that.*

Robert glanced away from his dance partner and caught Emerald's eye. She flushed, looking away, but almost immediately looked back. Her color deepened.

There was also a discomforting heat on his own cheeks.

Someone cleared their throat.

Robert blinked. The dance had moved on, though he had not moved with it. Sapphire was extending her hand and stub.

"You," he said, moving hastily, "are very perceptive. I did not expect you to be so."

Something disappeared from Sapphire's eyes, as though someone blew out the candle within her. "Because of my hand, I suppose," she said dully.

Robert cursed his phrasing. He could have explained that a lot better. "No, because you're so young."

He spoke easily, lightly, and just as easily, Sapphire perked up. "Oh. Oh, that's all Emerald. She has taught me so much about people watching—honestly, 'tis the most fascinating thing to do. The way she looks at people, she truly is so clever."

The dance took them further along the set, the movements demanding too much of their attention to permit either of them to speak for a moment, but when they came to rest, Sapphire continued immediately.

"And so beautiful, don't you think? Everyone said Coral was the prettiest—"

"Coral?"

"Our older sister," supplied Sapphire with a laugh. "But I think, truly, that Emerald has all the beauty. Don't you think?"

Robert smiled. Well, no one would be able to say that subtlety was a trait the youngest de Petras had, but then, it was endearing. If he'd had a younger sibling, he would have liked them to be like her.

"You really want me to marry her, don't you?" he said with a laugh.

It had been intended as a jest, but too late, Robert saw Emerald's sister was deadly serious.

"Of course," she said simply. "Don't you want to?"

# CHAPTER SEVEN

*May 5, 1810*

*THE FOURTH BALL.*

"I am sure it is not necessary for me to stay beyond a single dance," Emerald said helplessly.

Her fingers were gripping the seat of the carriage so hard, she was certain she might pull apart the stuffing.

She swallowed, thankful in the darkness Jasper de Petras was unable to see her fear.

Not that her father would be surprised. Why, it was he who had been so understanding, so kind, so patient when Sapphire had announced she had a headache that afternoon.

"A headache?" Opal had said lightly from the pianoforte. "Such a shame, Sapphy. Perhaps it will be best if you do not attend the ball tonight."

"A headache?" Emerald had repeated.

Fear had flooded her veins. A ball without Sapphire? Though she of course would hate being there even if her sister accompanied her, at least with her presence there was a buffer of sorts between her and the world.

Sapphire could speak to people. Sapphire could laugh, flutter her fan, smile.

And Emerald could merely stand beside her, ticking off another ball from her internal list, praying for the thing to be over soon. But if her sister did not accompany her…

"I really think it may be best, worse luck," Sapphire had said by the door. "I think I'll go upstairs and—"

"No!"

Emerald had flushed as both her parents and her sister looked at her. Even Captain, snoozing on a cushion, looked up to see what all the fuss was about. And Emerald had swallowed, tried desperately to frame her words on her tongue as clearly as they were in her mind…but it was impossible. When she had eventually spoken, it had been a rush of noise she herself had barely understood.

"But no, Sapphy, I need—ball, accompany me!"

Sapphire had lifted a hand to her head, and Emerald had to admit it did appear the youngest de Petras truly suffered. "But Ems, my head hurts…"

The carriage lurched. Jasper shifted in the seat opposite her, but Emerald had not moved a jot.

*They must be almost there. Her fourth ball.*

Almost halfway through her agreement with her mother, Emerald attempted to remind herself. After this ball, there were only six more to go. And then she would be free.

"Really I should have stayed behind to care of Sapphire," Emerald said aloud, suddenly struck by genius. "We should turn the carriage around, Papa, so I can—"

"Avoid going to a ball?" Jasper chuckled in the darkness of the carriage. "Emerald, please. I am not so old and decrepit that I cannot tell when you are merely attempting to avoid this darned ball—and yes, before you say anything, I have no real wish to go either."

"Then why can't we—"

"Because I made a promise to your mother, and you made an agreement with her, and neither of us are brave enough to argue with her," came the wry reply.

Emerald had to smile ruefully. Her father was not wrong, at

least, not entirely wrong.

Opal de Petras was a very approachable woman, patient with her children, most of the time, and a good friend, from what Emerald could see.

But she was the head of the household. All her children had taken her name, and though their father's shipping business provided the healthy income the family enjoyed of just over two thousand a year, it was their mother's fortune that provided for their dowries.

Emerald's stomach lurched. *Dowries.*

As if she was in need of such a thing!

Emerald swallowed. She was not going to think about him. It was utterly impossible that he will be attending this ball, after all, far too common for a marquess. A public ball!

Her mother, indeed, had been a little surprised when Emerald had agreed to attend tonight as one of her ten.

"But it's—well, a public ball, absolutely anyone could—"

"Precisely," Emerald had cut across her with a shy smile. "So no one will know me there. Just what I want."

The carriage started to slow and Jasper stretched, sighing. "Ten balls, and you had to lumber me with this one."

"Father!"

"Well, there won't be anyone to play cards with, that's all I'm saying."

It did not matter. The mere suggestion that she had chosen ill was enough to flare panic in Emerald's chest.

What if the place was full of ruffians? What if she was unable to find someone to speak with? Worse, what if someone spoke to her and forced her to dance…

An image flashed through Emerald's mind as she tried not to think about just how many people would be inside, waiting for her.

Robert. The Marquess of Swindmore, as she would have to remember to call him. The way he'd looked at her when dancing with Sapphire…it was unfathomably strange. What had been even more strange was the way her heart had pattered painfully just looking at him dancing with her sister.

Which was ridiculous, Emerald told herself as the carriage came to a halt and she steeled herself. She was not jealous of Sapphire, never had been. In a family of three such different sisters, they were fortunate to rarely compare themselves to each other.

No, it was something about seeing a woman, any woman, dancing with Robert.

Perhaps she should have agreed to dance with him, after all.

Emerald firmly pushed the thought from her mind as she was helped out of the carriage by her father's steady hand. No, she would not think of him. Even if she hoped the marquess would be here tonight.

Emerald blinked. Her father was looking at her with great concern, and it was only then that she realized she had been standing there for at least a minute without saying a word.

She smiled weakly. "We really could just go home, you know."

A strange look passed across her father's face. It was not disappointment, and it was certainly not rage. It was not frustration, but it was close—yet there was understanding there Emerald had never seen before.

"You truly are my daughter."

Emerald frowned. "I beg your pardon?"

"Your mother," he said heavily, "is a social butterfly. She enjoys the Season, she enjoys dances and card parties, and all those things. I do not."

Emerald stared. It was unbelievable; her father always loved attending the various invitations the de Petras family received.

"You…you do not?"

"One thing you will soon learn, little one—"

"Papa!"

"—is that being an adult often means doing things one does not like."

Emerald sighed. "To impress others."

"To give yourself options."

The evening was dark, but she could still make out her father's face. Emerald had never seen him look like that, as though he was telling her something vital, something new.

"Scandal will hit each and every family in the *ton* at one point or another, that is a certainty," said Jasper in a low voice as people dressed in their finery walked past, chattering away about the ball. "The families which survive are those who have enough credit, enough friends, friends in the right places—options, in short."

Emerald swallowed. A memory trickled into her mind—a journey to the house of Lady Romeril when scandal had hit the de Petras family when she had been very young.

Other memories followed: Lady Romeril beaming and welcoming them into her home; Lady Romeril ensuring her mother received an invitation to the best parties...Lady Romeril requesting to be Sapphire's godmother...

"Lady Romeril," she breathed.

Jasper laughed. "Perhaps not my choice, but Opal chose well. Lady Romeril helped our family regain respectability, and your mother, of course, but without that option..."

Emerald stared, not entirely understanding what he was trying to tell her. "Do you...do you mean to say that you believe there will be another time, in the future, when the de Petras family will require help to stay respectable?"

It was a worrying thought. Why, they received more than enough attention merely by being the de Petras family, Emerald hating every moment of it. *The idea of more...*

"All I am saying," said Jasper briskly, turning and offering her his arm, "is that attending these balls, though it is merely an agreement between you and your mother, should be viewed as useful. Each ball an opportunity. If you make it so."

Emerald's head swam as they stepped inside and were hit with a blast of noise, light, and heat.

*Useful?* Did her father know something she did not—did that whisper she and Micah had heard just weeks ago hold any truth?

*"I heard the mother gained her fortune through stealth or some criminal activity—"*

"Ah, your lordship," said Jasper pleasantly.

Emerald flinched but saw in an instant that it was not Robert.

Not that she wished it to be, she told herself fiercely as she stood and her father made polite conversation with the gentleman who had approached them. She should not consider Robert a gentleman, one whose company she should seek.

He was a marquess, and that meant, surely, he was a rake. He had to be. A gentleman who looked like that, spoke like that, had to know his way around the ladies.

"—course I will join you," her father's words rang in her ears. "Emerald will not mind, will you?"

Emerald stared as he removed his hand from hers and was starting to walk toward the card room. "Papa, wait—"

It was too late.

Emerald swallowed, forcing down the panic threatening to rise as she stood alone in a ballroom. *Alone. Entirely alone.*

Surely everyone was staring at her. Did that person glance at her? Was he whispering now to a friend?

A wash of dizziness overcame Emerald, and she took a sudden step to the left as though that would balance her, but the ballroom was still spinning. She had to do something, anything, but precisely what she could—

A woman in a deep red gown and two large feathers stepped to the side, revealing a gentleman she recognized.

Robert Ainsworth, Marquess of Swindmore.

Emerald did not think. Thinking was for those who did not have panic twisting their stomach or fear aching in their bones.

She stepped forward, ignoring those she passed, pushing aside a footman most rudely and not stopping to hear his piteous complaints now that a bottle of wine had slopped over his waistcoat, and strode right up to Robert.

"Talk to me," Emerald said breathlessly.

Robert raised an eyebrow. "I beg your pardon?"

She would not beg, almost certainly, but Emerald did not know what else to do. If he was talking to her, the world would leave her alone, wouldn't it? There would be no awkward sympathetic looks, no mutters that her elder sister had been far more interesting at parties, nothing like that.

As long as he spoke to her.

"Talk to me," Emerald said, her eyes not leaving his as her heart beat furiously in her chest. "About anything."

He did not understand her. How could she make him see?

Despite her better judgment, Emerald reached out and took his hand. Hers shook, freezing even in the heat of the ballroom, and Robert's eyes widened at the sudden contact.

"Please," Emerald breathed.

Her traitorous heart started to slow. A peace came upon her, something wrenching the tension from her shoulders. That made it easier to breathe, and with every breath came calm.

Emerald stared at the man before her. How did he do this? How did one simple touch calm her, remove the anxiety swimming in her mind and, instead, replace it with peace?

Robert's fingers tightened around hers, and her heart started to race again. Emerald swallowed, tensing her shoulders, prepared for the waves of panic to return...

But they did not. This was something different, quite different to the fear that typically overtook her at a ball. Almost...enjoyable.

"My word, Miss de Petras," Robert breathed. "You are a marvel."

Emerald tried to smile weakly. What had possessed her to do such a forward thing, she could not fathom, but it seemed to have worked.

At least, no one was staring at her with pity now. They were probably astonished at her touching a gentleman so boldly, but that was a different kind of gossip, one she could weather. For now.

"Emerald," said Robert in a low voice, "I was wondering—would you like to—"

"Absolutely not," said Emerald firmly.

She tried to wrench her fingers from his but found they were held tight. She should have known this was a mistake—he had entirely misunderstood her plea for company and was now about to ask her to dance again!

*When would the man learn?*

But Robert did not appear offended by her swift rebuttal. If anything, he looked rather charmed. "You are a curious creature, you know that?"

She shivered. This intimacy, the like she had not expected, was too much—yet, in a way, she did not comprehend, not enough.

"I was going to ask you whether you wished to take a turn about the room."

She blinked up into his dark eyes and hesitated. A turn about the room. Well, it would certainly explain to the people watching why she had taken his hand—and it would give her a chance to survey the room for potential escape routes, the moment she considered herself to have "attended" the darn ball.

"Fine."

"You could at least pretend to enjoy my company," said Robert calmly, placing her hand on his arm and starting to walk.

Emerald almost stumbled. *Pretend?* She was doing enough pretending, all to ensure that she did not create a scandal. But was she inadvertently about to do the same thing?

"Emerald de Petras," said Robert quietly.

"What?"

Cringing at her rudeness, Emerald had no chance to say more because he continued.

"For such a beautiful woman, I am astonished how little you enjoy being looked at."

Cheeks searing with heat, Emerald tried not to think about

the words that had just come from his mouth. What on earth did Robert think he was playing at!

"I hate being looked at," she said coldly as they reached a corner of the room and turned to walk along the next wall.

"I know." Robert's voice was not accusatory. It was, if anything, kind. "You hate being watched by Society, you fear gossip. I can see it in your eyes. Feel it in your fingers."

Emerald unconsciously clenched her fingers on his arm, then tried to relax.

Relax? While walking arm in arm with a marquess around a ballroom where surely everyone would be—

"Why?"

"Why what?"

He shrugged. "Why everything. Why do you hate it so much?"

What an odd question to ask. It was like attempting to describe the color blue or the way a cool breeze made all the hair on the back of one's neck rise up. It was the salt in the air by the sea, the way a smile from a mother healed most wounds.

Emerald swallowed. How did one put such things into words? "I...I do not..."

She could feel the panic rising now, but just then she caught Robert's eye.

He was not laughing. He was not teasing, mocking, anything like what she had expected. In truth, he looked rather...interested. Curious.

Emerald cleared her throat. She would be mistress of herself. "My family...we have not always been as respectable as we are now. My father...he disappeared."

"Disappeared?"

Her gaze had dropped to her skirts, but Emerald forced herself to look up and saw nothing but interest on Robert's face. Her gaze flittered to his jaw, the way his sideburns—

Emerald tried to smile. "He was gone seven years. My mother actually had him declared dead—a complete misunderstanding of—"

"Declared dead?"

"And they had to marry again, but not after my mother considered leaving him—"

"Your mother?"

Emerald smiled ruefully. "Still wish to take a turn about the room with me?"

Robert halted. "No."

It was not the answer she had been expecting. Disappointment rushed through Emerald's heart as Robert released her hand, and the separation from the handsome man, one so charming as to actually convince her to walk about the room with her…

Now it was over. She had frightened him off.

"Oh," Emerald said helplessly.

A smile crept across Robert's lips, and when he spoke, it was in a low voice. "Oh, I want to do far more than take a turn about the room with you."

"Wh—What on earth are you—"

But Emerald was not permitted enough breath to continue. Robert had grabbed her hand and pulled her through a door, slamming it behind him. The noise of the ball—the music, the laughter, the chatter—all became muffled.

They were standing in a much smaller room, perhaps used as a tearoom or card room. A few candles only lit the place. It was dark, far darker than the dazzling ballroom.

Emerald swallowed. She was alone in a dark room with a gentleman who was a rake.

"Now," said Robert, stepping so close Emerald had to tilt her head to hold his gaze. "Now we are going to do something I have wanted to do the moment I first laid eyes on you."

Emerald's breath caught in her throat. He was going to kiss her. He was going to kiss her and the worst of it all was that she wanted him to! How was she going to stop herself from falling in love with a man who wanted to kiss her!

"Y-You are?"

Robert nodded. Emerald tried not to look at those lips but it was impossible; they danced tantalizingly just above her.

"One, two, three, four…" he breathed. He closed his eyes.

Emerald could not help herself. Her eyelashes fluttered, eyes closing, but no welcome warmth, no expected pressure pressed down on her lips. Instead, she heard footsteps.

Opening her eyes in a hurry, she saw the most odd sight she had ever seen in her life. Robert was…dancing.

At least, almost. His eyes closed, he was stepping along to the faint strains of the music, managing to creep under the door, his hands out as though expecting her to join him.

"You cannot be serious," Emerald breathed.

Robert grinned, eyes still shut. "You don't like being looked at, and I want to dance with you. I thought this a particularly convenient compromise."

"Compromise?"

There he stood, the most handsome, most charming man she had ever met, one who appeared unfazed by her family's…well, her family. And he wanted to dance with her. Even if that meant doing it with his eyes closed.

Emerald took a hesitant step forward, then paused. What was she doing?

She had vowed she would never be married, would never suffer eyes staring, and the wife of a marquess would surely be in the eyes of Society far more than she was now.

But there was something about him. Robert. He drew her to him, and as he turned as the dance dictated, for the first time in her life, Emerald let go.

She joined him. Her hands met his, and Robert gasped, the intensity of their connection too much, and she luxuriated in the way he clearly wished to open his eyes—but did not.

His footsteps were joined by hers. Emerald tried not to think, just to feel, the rhythm of the music, the sway of the steps, the way his hands met hers—and it was glorious, it was far more than she could ever have imagined.

When was the last time she had danced like this? Had she ever danced in public, beyond her family? Not that she could remember.

"You are a wonderful dancer," murmured Robert.

Emerald giggled. "You can't see me!"

"I don't need to see you," he countered. "I have a perfect image of you right—here."

She had expected him to point to his eyes, his head perhaps, or if he was going to be utterly ridiculous, his heart—but Robert did something far more unexpected.

In a swift movement, far more impressive considering he had his eyes shut, Emerald was swept into his arms. Robert's hands were on her waist, clinging onto her, pulling her close, and she gasped as her breasts pressed up against his very solid chest.

They stood there, Emerald's heart racing, for what felt like forever. She should pull away, knew it was madness to stand here, madness! But she wanted to stand here, wanted to feel him. Be felt by him. Be seen by him in a way no one else ever had. Even with his eyes shut.

"Robert," Emerald breathed.

His eyes flickered open, and there was something desperate and dark in his eyes as he beheld her. "Emerald."

This was it this time, she was almost certain. Emerald could feel the desire pouring from him, desire for her, and it was matched by something in her that was stirring, stirring beyond what she could bear!

Just as she tilted her head toward him, welcoming in the kiss she was sure would follow, the door behind her banged open.

Emerald lurched from Robert's arms and spluttered, "L-Lady Romeril!"

Lady Romeril beamed as Emerald saw, out of the corner of her eye, Robert hastily stepping back. "My word, Miss Emerald de Petras. I never thought I'd see the day."

# CHAPTER EIGHT

*May 9, 1810*

*T*HE FIFTH BALL.

Almack's appeared to be designed, from what Robert could tell, to be intensely discomforting to all who were there.

Standing as he was in the entrance hallway, Robert could see into the ballroom and two of the rooms. Everyone in both locations looked remarkably uncomfortable.

Robert smiled wryly. At least no one appeared to be having as good a time as he'd had with Miss Emerald de Petras the other evening, and he had been dancing with his eyes shut.

Not that it had mattered. The face and figure of that tempting woman were seared into his mind.

Robert shifted awkwardly on his feet as one of the footmen stared.

It was rather odd, even he had to admit, for a gentleman to loiter about the place, but then he had to be sure that he found Emerald the moment she arrived.

If she was coming.

Of course, she was.

Emerald would be here. She was certain to be. Though he was only now starting to understand her—that story she told about her parents was most astonishing and would certainly explain why she disliked attention—Robert was not so arrogant as to think he had her entirely worked out.

But if he was any judge, Emerald would make the most of an Almack's night where the same dull people came every Wednesday. She would receive no questions, no awkward comments, and Robert was going to take advantage of that.

At least, he hoped to. The plan he had concocted in the early hours of that morning had seemed perfect, but now he stood here, waiting for a family to arrive which may never come, he was starting to feel…

Well. A bit foolish.

It was not a good idea to be seen courting a young lady who not only had a murky familial past of her own but had no desire to be married!

Not that he wanted to marry her. Robert tried to push the thought from his mind as he shifted his feet. Matrimony was absolutely out of the question, for he'd had enough of the thing for a lifetime.

He wanted to seduce her. Wanted to get Emerald de Petras under him—or on top of him, if he was very lucky—feel the pleasure and ache of her, then move on. Leave her behind.

He needed pleasure, not heartbreak.

"—so busy this time of year, I really think—"

His heart leapt. Was that the de Petras family?

A gaggle of people entered, and Robert's shoulders slumped as he recognized none of them. He should go home, leave London, and avoid whatever mischief he was about to get himself and Emerald entangled in. At least, that would be the clever thing to do.

Goodness, he was in danger, then. No, the best thing he could do was seduce Emerald as soon as possible, get her out of his system, and then move on. The dance with his eyes closed had been a laugh, at first, a way to show her he was not a stick in the mud as so many in Society were.

But it had become more than that.

In the silence of Almack's entrance hall, Robert tried not to think of the heady intensity that had swept his body as he had danced with an unseen but definitely felt Emerald. The way her hands had met his—hesitant at first, then bold, the boldness he had known within her emerging as she felt safe.

*Safe with him.* The woman had no idea what—

"Robert?"

Robert started and saw Emerald de Petras, flushing as she spoke his first name, and saw with mingled delight and frustration that she was here. She was here!

She was also with—

"Robert, is it?" said Sapphire de Petras with a grin. "How marvelous."

"Your lordship, how pleasant to see you again," said Opal de Petras, rushing toward him and curtseying. "You have not met my other daughter, I do not think, Coral de Petras, and her husband—"

"You're the marquess, then?" said a woman with red hair as she arched an eyebrow, stepping forward and leaving Emerald to flush behind her. "You are not at all what I expected."

"Coral!"

"Oh, Mama, I am sure the gentleman is not offended," said Coral with a laugh.

"No, his lordship is not easily offended," said Sapphire confidently as Robert merely gaped at the lot of them. "Why, once Micah said—"

"Micah has a particular way with words I would not wish upon anyone," said a gentleman Robert did not know. "Duke of Glaenarm, part of this rabble despite my better judge—"

"Do not even say such things, Edward, you cannot take them back!"

Robert stared, dazzled by the onslaught of the de Petras family—and not all of them were there! The son and father were absent, as far as he could tell, though the ladies were more than enough.

"—not shout at him, you're not at home now Coral—"

"Edward doesn't mind how I speak to him, and I'll thank you, Sapphy, to keep out—"

"Girls, really!"

Robert stepped to the right, and the most beautiful woman he had ever seen came back into view.

He did not think. Thinking was not necessary. His instincts overtook him, propelling him toward Emerald—before he was accosted by the eldest daughter.

"Your lordship," said Coral sternly. "Just what are your intentions toward my sister?"

"Coral!" Emerald hissed, her silence finally broken by sheer embarrassment.

"Is that not my job to ask?" said Opal haughtily. "I don't know, this generation—"

"Oh, things are changing, Mama, and you cannot stop them," Sapphire said brightly. She winked at Robert. "Why, I have considered wearing breeches to my next ball, I heard that Miss Seton—"

"Breeches to a ball!"

Robert watched, amazed, as Sapphire grinned at the raucous argument she had created. All eyes of the family were on her— *expertly done*, he thought as he stepped to Emerald.

He should not do it. He knew that, knew the plan he had pulled together simply could not move forward.

*Matrimony.* Oh, none of them had said it, as their voices raised around him and the argument spilled out, but he could see it in their eyes.

Robert Ainsworth, Marquess of Swindmore, was now considered the potential suitor for Emerald de Petras, that was plain. If he were clever, he would back away, politely leave, and ensure he was never seen in public with her again.

After all, he had raised expectations he could not fill. *Would not.*

He would not be proposing marriage to anyone, let alone

Emerald de Petras.

"I do apologize for them," said Emerald quietly.

Robert jumped. So lost in his thoughts, he had hardly noticed his feet had drifted him closer and closer to the woman he was fast becoming…well, not obsessed with.

He had been obsessed with Isabelle. A dark, blinding obsession that had prevented him from seeing the truth. This was different. Deeper somehow. Yet lighter.

"Apologize?" Robert said lightly.

Emerald smiled ruefully. "My family is a little…well, intense is not strong enough."

He had to chuckle. "Oh, I don't know what you could mean…"

Robert allowed his voice to trail off as he glanced meaningfully over his shoulder. Sapphire was laughing, saying something under her breath he could not make out, and Coral was actually having to be held back by her husband. The mother stood in the middle, hands raised, as though trying to placate two bulls.

"I love them dearly, but they are…well. A bit much," said Emerald as she removed her pelisse and offered it to a waiting footman.

Robert did not think. Once again instincts took over, and this time, he let them. This was the perfect opportunity to have Emerald to himself and explain…certainly not the truth, by no means.

A chance to let her down gently, then. A chance to explain that whatever she or her family hoped from him, he could certainly not give it to them.

Robert reached out and took the pelisse himself. "Come on."

Emerald blinked. "I beg your pardon?"

He did not reply with words. Carefully placing the pelisse back around her shoulders as the de Petras family argued—and trying not to shiver at the contact as his fingertips brushed against her shoulders—Robert grabbed Emerald's hand and pulled her toward the door.

Not the door to the ballroom. *Oh no.*

"Robert, we cannot leave!"

"Of course we can," he said cheerfully, stepping out into the balmy spring night air. "There is no law that says a person cannot leave Almack's!"

"Robert, you are wild!" Emerald was giggling, her cheeks pinking at his odd behavior, but she had not turned back to Almack's. "Where do you think you're going?"

"Anywhere."

"Anywhere?"

His gaze met Emerald's, and an inexplicable moment passed between them.

As though they were meant to be here. As though his entire life had led up to this point. As though by accident, chance, or fate, the world had conspired to have him with her.

Emerald pulled him onto the pavement, and he refused to allow her free of his hands.

"What is going on in that mind of yours?" she whispered.

Robert swallowed. It was an excellent question, not one he felt able to answer.

It was not his head, after all, that was in control here. Oh no, it was other parts of him. His heart. His manhood, a little. But most of all his chest, tight with pain whenever he was not with her and soaring whenever he had hold of her hands. *Or her waist…*

"We," Robert said quietly, "are going to abandon Almack's."

"Abandon—you cannot be serious!" Emerald's green eyes were wide.

Robert could not completely understand the emotion in those green eyes, but he did not need to. Did they mirror his own? Did she know, even suspect, what she did to him?

Lord, just having her this close to him, hand in hand, in public, was enough to—

"Why not?" Robert said, self-assurance throbbing in his words. "Are you afraid?"

"Afraid?" Emerald certainly did not sound afraid. "Not of you."

*"Not of you."*

Robert almost groaned to hear her words. Oh, she was a dark horse, this one. At one moment wallflower, the next, something quite different.

"This is my fifth ball," she said. "My agreement with my mother, I must attend—"

"And you did," he said, starting to walk down the road. Anything to get away from Almack's, from the noise, from the fear that someone at any point could come out and see them...see him with her...

Emerald laughed wryly as she followed him. "You can explain that to my mother."

"I don't think I would dare," Robert admitted, his heart racing.

She laughed again, and his heart soared, skipping a beat as he watched the joy on her face—a sight all too rare. What he wouldn't give to make Emerald de Petras smile every day...

"You are certainly a contrary debutante," said Robert as they turned a corner onto a quieter road. "That is what your family calls you, is it not?"

Emerald shook her head. "Oh, you are much mistaken if you still believe me a debutante! That was years ago."

He saw the pain in her eyes, the way her shoulders immediately tensed. There was hurt there, hurt he did not understand but wanted to.

Unpicking Emerald, unraveling all that made her who she was...it would be a gift, an honor. Something for a man far better than him, Robert told himself sternly. It was not as though he had any serious intentions toward her...

"You are still contrary though," he pointed out.

Emerald sighed, though a smile lingered. "I suppose I am, in a way. Perhaps that is the true family characteristic of my siblings and me. We are all contrary in our own ways."

"Yet I am still to meet a woman who is…well. Contrary to the point of restricting herself from pleasure."

The words had slipped out before Robert could stop them. He was right, he knew it, but perhaps those words were not precisely the ones he should have used.

A faint flush streaked across Emerald's cheeks, but she did not halt, did not declare she would have to leave him after such a thing.

His heart twisted, desire melting into a pool in his stomach, then a little lower. How long had it been since he'd had a woman? Six months? Longer? It was impossible to believe he had lasted this long, but it was not just desperation that drew him to Emerald.

"I hoped you would be at Almack's tonight," he confessed.

"You did?"

Was that eagerness in her eyes? Robert could hardly tell, hardly knew whether he was coming or going. When was the last time a woman had had this effect on him?

*Isabelle? No, this was different.*

"I had hoped you would favor me with a dance," Robert said, allowing a teasing lilt into his tone. "Not in public, of course."

"What, with your eyes shut?" Emerald giggled. "I admit, I am impressed you did not fall."

"So am I," he said.

They turned another corner, this time onto a deserted street.

Lust poured through Robert as he breathed in the cooling night air. This would be the perfect place, if he had decided to do what he knew he certainly should not.

Because Emerald de Petras was not the flighty chit of a woman he'd had in mind for a short seduction, was she? No, she had a family who would be remarkably pleased to have him as a son-in-law, from what he could see. A family who would not hesitate to protect her honor if he decided to stain it.

A rush of eagerness almost caused Robert to trip. By God, he wanted to stain it. Wanted to kiss her lips, claim her innocence as no one else could.

"I had thought…I mean, at the ball…I was certain you were going to…"

Robert halted, and Emerald stood beside him, her hand slipping from his arm, and it was like a bereavement to have her apart from him.

Her eyes were wide, lips unmoving but parted, and Robert almost groaned aloud to see the look she gave him.

He knew what she was going to say; he did not need to hear the precise words, though they would be sweet and far too seductive to hear. She had thought he was going to kiss her.

If Lady Romeril had not disturbed them, Robert thought darkly, he probably would have. Which was ridiculous. He should not be kissing a lady like Emerald de Petras; he certainly should not be taking her on unchaperoned midnight walks…

So, what was he doing here?

Emerald swallowed. Robert tried not to watch her throat move, his gaze moving lower to the untouched softness of her décolletage.

A throbbing pulse of desire rocked him.

"I thought…" Emerald licked her lips, and Robert's eyes flickered to them as she resolved to speak. "When we were dancing. I thought you were going to kiss me."

Robert hesitated. There was only one direction this conversation should go, shared here in the dead of night, alone. Only one direction a gentleman should go, and that was straight back to Almack's. *Take her back to her family*, a part of him cried, *before it's too late!*

"I wanted to," he breathed, not looking away. "But I would not wish to give rise to any…any expectations."

Emerald said nothing for a moment. Then she stepped forward, closing the distance between them, and Robert almost groaned aloud to have such delectable temptation so close.

"I told you before, I do not wish to be married," she whispered. "But that does not mean…do you want to kiss me now?"

And that was it. Robert had been restrained, no one could charge him otherwise, but that was too much.

Moaning as he pulled her into his arms, Robert lowered his lips onto Emerald's and almost wept with their sweetness, the innocence, and yet the desperate eagerness for pleasure as she parted them, welcoming him in.

The kiss deepened. Robert knew he should stop, knew it was madness, utter madness, but the confidence that neither of them desired matrimony yet wanted each other was enough to open the floodgates of his desire.

Emerald quivered in his arms, moaned in his mouth as Robert teased her tongue with his own, and his breathing sharpened, quickened, as the kiss melted him into her arms.

And then it was over.

Robert stepped back, heart racing, hardly able to believe he had managed to stop there. Just on the gates of seduction.

"I think," he said jaggedly, knowing he would regret this later but also knowing this was the only thing an honorable man could do, "I should take you back to Almack's now."

Emerald's lips were still parted, and there was a strange hazy look in her eyes. The look of one who has, for the first time, tasted pleasure.

"To be sure, that is what a debutante would do," she whispered, refusing to look away as a shy smile crept across her face. "But I am a contrary one, remember?"

As Robert sank into another kiss, hardly needing any other invitation, two thoughts flashed through his mind.

Firstly, that he was in great danger of making Emerald de Petras fall in love with him.

Secondly, that he was in great danger of falling in love himself.

And then the heady pleasure of the kiss overwhelmed him, and he succumbed to Emerald's embrace.

# CHAPTER NINE

*May 10, 1810*

"—BUT, OF COURSE, he remembered, and the room was absolutely festooned with roses! I told him, Edward, this is far too much money to spend on roses when they will only last a few days, and what do you think he said?"

Emerald blinked. The onslaught of words had been difficult to keep track of, but it appeared she was being asked her opinion.

Coral was glaring. "Ems, are you even listening to me?"

"Yes? Yes!" Emerald said hastily, pulling a cushion onto her lap, as though it could act as a shield against her talkative and rather domineering sister. "What did you ask me?"

Coral rolled her eyes as only an elder sibling could when not being given all the attention. "Emerald, surely it is not too much to ask that you pay attention to the conversation we are having?"

It sounded like a small thing when her sister put it like that, but Emerald was not sure it was so simple.

After all, Coral had not been officially invited to the de Petras home, and that meant no one knew she was coming. Sapphire was somewhere, no one knew where, and Micah was staying at his lodgings again. The last argument with their father had been terrible to behold. Opal was out visiting, of course, and that left…

"Emerald! Can you hear me?"

Emerald jumped and smiled weakly at her sister. "I can hear you."

Coral sighed. "I do not know how you manage it, really, Ems! It is as though you simply swan through life, expecting everyone else to pick up the slack of conversation!"

"That is not fair," said Emerald quietly.

She would have put up more of a fight if she thought her sister likely to listen, but Coral had never been one for listening to another person. It was her way or no way at all.

"Oh, nothing's fair when it comes to you," said Coral, throwing up her hands and leaning back. The drawing room was bathed with light. "As I was saying—Edward had purchased an inordinate number of roses, and I was telling him what a waste of money it was. Waste, he said to me, how can it be a waste? When I have a wife as beautiful as you…"

Emerald did try this time, she really did. As Coral prattled on about her husband, how wonderful he was, how marriage was perfect and everyone should wish to be within it—definitely a speech their mother had asked her to give, Emerald thought wryly—it became increasingly difficult to pay attention.

It was not as though Emerald did not like her brother-in-law. Edward was…fine, as gentlemen went. No, perhaps that was not fair. Emerald clutched the cushion, enjoying its comforting protective warmth, and nodded as Coral continued.

"—five whole guineas, and I told him that was simply not possible, we would have to look for another supplier if he could not reduce his rates—"

Edward was pleasant enough in conversation, direct enough with her sister to be palatable, and a duke, which was a slight disadvantage. Emerald could not recall being so looked at as when she accompanied Coral, the new Duchess of Glaenarm, about the place.

But it was not Coral's fault, really, that she was so in love. Emerald could see that, saw the heightened expression of affection on her sister's cheeks whenever she spoke of him.

It was a love match, and that was a rare and precious thing indeed in this day and age.

But Emerald simply could not bear sitting through what felt like hours and hours of praise of her brother-in-law. Surely no one could stand it?

"—because matrimony is the very best thing for one's happiness," Coral was saying, her cheeks flushed and her eyes bright. "You know I had very specific parameters for my husband, of course, and it is quite right for a woman to have high expectations. Why, I have said several times to Edward, if he had not met them…"

Emerald nodded. Not that she agreed. It was ridiculous, the entire thing. If one did not *have* to get married, why bother?

*"I told you before, I do not wish to be married. But that does not mean…do you want to kiss me now?"*

Heat scalded her face, and she dropped her gaze to the cushion in her lap as Captain snuffled, sleeping alongside her on the sofa.

She was not going to think about him. Robert. No, she wouldn't even think his name, for once again heat rushed through her body at the mere thought of him.

*Him.* The gentleman who had given her a first kiss—and a second…and a third.

Just how long they had stood in that street, kissing furiously, as though their lives would end if they did anything so foolish as to let go…

Emerald swallowed, trying not to think about last night and yet utterly unable to push it from her mind. She should not have done it. She had been forward, far more forward than ever before, and it was ridiculous to have permitted herself when she knew she had no heart for matrimony.

"—and as a wife, I think it only right I tell you—where are you going?"

Emerald smiled nervously. She had risen to her feet, unable to take any more of her sister's lecture, but unfortunately had not considered much beyond that. "Out."

"Out?" repeated Coral, all amazement. "What do you mean, out?"

Emerald gestured to the sunshine pouring through the windows. "Out, Coral. Not here."

Her sister's eyes narrowed. "You're just trying to avoid me, aren't you? It's about that gentleman, that Marquess of Swindmore. Where were you at Almack's yesterday, none of us could find you, and the last time I saw you, you were talking to—"

"I need to take Captain out for her walk," Emerald said hastily.

Hopefully, her sister would take her blushes as just the typical look she always had when disagreeing with someone. The last thing she needed was for Coral to think her affected color was anything to do with...

Emerald swallowed. *Robert Ainsworth, Marquess of Swindmore.* Ainsworth. It was a nice name. If she were to be married—and she had no intention of being married, so it did not matter—but if she were going to be married, Ainsworth was a nice name.

Not that it mattered. In the de Petras household, ladies kept their names. Coral had even suggested giving hers to the duke, which had caused a great stir and many comments in Society, for which Emerald had never forgiven her.

"Captain?" blinked Coral.

The dog raised her head at the sound of her name, and Emerald beamed at her pet. That was the wonderful thing about having a dog. Everyone could look at the dog, not her.

"Captain," she said firmly. "The poor thing has been inside all day, and she needs—"

"Oh, a walk will do splendidly," said Coral, rising to her feet—much to Emerald's horror. "I have felt the need for a—"

"N-No," stammered Emerald.

The two sisters stood there, Coral's mouth open, Emerald's jaw tightly shut.

Oh, this was such a nightmare! Was she ever to be given the

courtesy of solitude?

"No?" Coral repeated, her eyes narrowing.

If she was not careful, Emerald was going to spend the entire afternoon being lectured by her sister about the benefits of matrimony, story after story of how happy she was with Edward, punctuated with dire warnings about what happened to old maids.

She had to do something. *Anything!*

"I thought I would mull over your—your wise words," Emerald attempted, trying to smile. "You have given me a great deal to think about, Coral, and I wish to give it the time and attention it deserves."

Her breath halted in her lungs as she waited for her sister's response. Surely Coral was not that foolish as to believe—

"Well, I must say, that is progress," said Coral smartly, settling herself back on the sofa with a delighted smile. "Good. Think it all over, Emerald, for I am sure you will swiftly come to understand my—"

"I will think it over," interrupted Emerald, hardly sure how she was so daring, and with Coral, too! "Thank you."

In less than a minute, she was walking along the pavement with Captain on her lead, trotting just ahead of her, eagerly sniffing everything that came in her path.

Emerald took a deep breath and felt the tension slowly dissipate from her body. How long had it been since she was truly on her own? In all honesty, she could hardly remember. There was always someone telling her to do something, indicating she should be different, consider another gentleman for a dance, for a conversation, for matrimony…

Captain sniffled, returned to Emerald's heel, then darted forward again.

A smile crept across Emerald's face. A walk, with her dog. No expectations, no conversation required.

The sunshine played with the leaves on the trees of Hyde Park as Emerald entered it, dancing light and shadows across the paths. Nothing could ruin the solitude…

"Miss de Petras!"

Emerald froze. Captain yapped, unsure why they had stopped, but she could not attend to her. She could not attend to anything. She knew that voice. Knew it better than she was starting to know her own. After all, she tried to speak as little as possible, whereas he—

"Miss de Petras!" Robert had run over to her—actually run!— and put a hand to his chest as he panted, slightly out of breath. "I thought it was you. I wanted to shout Emerald, but I managed to contain myself."

She smiled weakly.

*"I told you before, I do not wish to be married. But that does not mean…do you want to kiss me now?"*

It was all she could think about, all she could see. The sensations of that moment crowded her mind, making it impossible to think of anything else.

Robert's hands on her waist, his lips on hers, the way his tongue—

"Are you quite well?"

Emerald swallowed. Robert was looking at her with genuine concern.

And that was because she had not spoken. Emerald knew she had to speak, had to say something. She could not just stand here with Captain barking eagerly between them, her lead getting tangled, and say nothing.

But what could she say? That she had made a terrible mistake last night—one never to be repeated? That she did not know what had come over her when she had said those words which made him kiss her, which made him cling to her in that way she never wanted to stop…

"I like your dog," said Robert cheerfully.

Emerald's gaze snapped to Captain, now sitting eagerly, hoping for a treat. "Dog."

"Well, I assume she is yours," Robert said, kneeling to pat the dog.

Captain barked happily and rolled over to present her stomach for scratches.

Emerald rolled her eyes. How was it possible that she had ended up with a dog who so adored other people? They could not have been more different.

It was strange, seeing the two of them together. Emerald's heart twisted. Robert and Captain, clearly new friends if her dog could have anything to do with it. Two of the creatures in the world that she most cared about.

She forced the thought away. What about her family—her commitment never to marry?

Robert straightened up and spoke in a low voice as other visitors to Hyde Park promenaded around them. "I have not been able to stop thinking about that kiss, you know."

"Neither have I," she breathed. She needed to pull herself together—she needed to say the words she knew must be said. "And I apologize."

Robert's face froze. Evidently, he had not been expecting that. "Apologize? Dear God, why?"

Her body did not want to distance itself from Robert, which was most irritating, for her mind certainly did.

Didn't it?

"Because...well, I told you," she said wretchedly. "I have no wish to get married."

Robert looked at her closely, waiting for her to continue.

Oh, wasn't it obvious? Did he have to make her spell it out so awkwardly?

"I...oh, Robert, I am sorry," Emerald said, her voice catching in her throat. "I had no intention of giving you the wrong idea—of making you think that I—"

"The wrong idea—you are worried *you* have given *me* a false impression?" Robert laughed as he spoke, almost as though he was relieved.

It made no sense to Emerald. She attempted to understand

Robert's words.

Did he mean that he believed he had given her the wrong impression?

In a way, it would be rather convenient. The thought had first come to her last night, when she had slipped into the de Petras home and rushed up to her bedchamber, as though she was afeard she would be caught in some terrible embrace.

They had managed to stop kissing just as they had turned onto her street.

It would be convenient if she had to marry. Robert would be convenient, that is.

After all, Emerald knew little of him. The delicate inquiries she had made of Micah, on his last visit—her brother had not really taken in the man's name, save to say that he knew no ill of him.

And was that not rather perfect? A gentleman of good name, good fortune, who was rarely in Town? Emerald could not have concocted a better suitor for her if she had tried.

But she could not think that way, she knew she could not. He was a marquess.

A shiver rushed down Emerald's spine. A marquess, and that would make her a marchioness. Everyone would look at her as she entered rooms, they would be expected to visit Almack's all Season long...

*No. Absolutely not.*

"So, what you're saying is," Robert said slowly, as Captain snuffled her displeasure that they were ignoring her so thoroughly, "is that you do not wish me to kiss you again."

Emerald glanced around them, but thankfully he had spoken quietly enough that it did not appear anyone else had heard.

No matter that it was precisely the opposite of what she wanted.

"Yes," she lied firmly, trying her best to meet his eye.

Why did he have to have such a knowing look?

"Is that what you really want?" asked Robert quietly. "Because I am not sure it is, Emerald. I think you are so afraid to say what you really want, what desires linger on your heart, that you may go through your entire life never experiencing them."

Emerald swallowed. How did he do it? Peer straight into her heart?

"I-I don't know what you mean," she said helplessly.

For a moment, a heady moment, she was sure he was going to lean forward and kiss her again. In broad daylight! In Hyde Park!

But then the moment was over. Robert stepped back, almost tripping over Captain's lead, as she had tangled it in and out of his legs, and when he had disentangled himself, he grinned at Emerald.

"Fine," he said lightly. "We have a bargain then."

Emerald blinked. *That did not sound right.* "W-We do?"

Robert nodded. "I agree not to kiss you again."

The words fell bitterly into her soul, but there was nothing she could do about it. She had made a commitment to herself, and a spinster she would remain.

"Until you ask me to."

Emerald's head snapped up. "I beg your pardon?"

"As I said, I will not kiss you again until you ask me to," said Robert in a low, teasing voice. A smile danced across his lips. "I know you, Emerald de Petras. You will not be able to resist me for long."

"Oh, yes I will," said Emerald, feeling every inch the contrary debutante her mother had called her.

The cheek of it! Did the man think her so uncontrolled, so wild, so—so taken with his kisses that she would not be able to resist him?

Robert's smile flickered slightly as his gaze meandered from her eyes to her lips. Emerald's breath caught in her chest. The way he looked at her….as though he were undressing her with his eyes. As though nothing else mattered, nothing else existed, just the two of them here, alone.

Unconsciously, she started to lean forward. *Just a few inches…*

Captain yapped as Emerald stepped near her tail. It was enough to shake her to her senses.

Emerald glared at the grinning marquess. "You made me do that."

"I did nothing of the sort," said Robert, shrugging as his eyes danced. "You want to kiss me, that's all."

It was all she could do to stay calm, but she managed to say with almost complete equanimity, "I will never ask you to kiss me."

Robert shrugged and took a step back, and Emerald almost cried out, she loathed the distance it created between them. "Well, you know your own mind best, I am sure. I just think that one day…you will."

# CHAPTER TEN

*May 19, 1810*

ROBERT BREATHED IN the heady medley of leather, smoke, and brandy that had been spilled on a carpet last century and no one had quite managed to get out.

Well, if there was one place in the world that could be considered home from home, it was here.

The Dulverton Club. The club of choice for the Swindmores for…well, more generations than he could count. There was something remarkably comforting about the way he was welcome here.

Reaching for the door handle, Robert breathed in again with a lazy smile on his face as the fumes from the Smoking Room to his left wafted into the hall.

Yes, this had been an excellent idea. He had too easily permitted his mind to wander whenever he was out there, in the world. It was all that letter's fault.

He should never have opened it. The moment Miles, his butler, had placed it on his breakfast tray, Robert had recognized that handwriting in an instant.

The letter had been dripping in vile teasing, and Robert had burned it the moment he had finished it, but that did not prevent him from still seeing the words across his vision…

*Robert,*

*My goodness, still in Town! One would almost think that you could not escape me. I hear through the grapevine that you are paying court to a Miss de Petras—a bold move, considering the story of her mother, don't you think?*

*Murderous brothers, scandalous secrets, threatening letters… I wonder if you wish to associate with such people.*

*But then, you hardly have a clean slate, do you?*

*If you need me again, I'll always be willing to take you back. I am sure I can find it in my heart to forgive you.*

*I'll be seeing you, Robert. I will always be your—*

*Isabelle*

He couldn't stay inside after reading bilge like that. Take him back? She was the one who had betrayed him!

And the gossip she spread—Opal de Petras, a criminal brother! Absolute nonsense. One only had to look at the woman to see she was a paragon of virtue. And as for her daughters…

Emerald de Petras, all the de Petrases, they were far too good at mystifying, befuddling, confusing, and changing his mind for him, leaving him little choice in the matter.

*"Well, you know your own mind best, I am sure. I just think that one day…you will."*

"Sir?"

Robert stared at the footman. *Sir? Sir!* He was a marquess, damn it. He so rarely pulled rank that he had almost forgotten what it felt like, but it was certainly not something he had imagined he would have to do here. This was the Dulverton Club, for goodness' sake!

"Yes?" he said as coldly as he could manage.

The footman, in the club's dark blue livery, had the grace to look ashamed. "My lord."

"That's better," said Robert haughtily. The tone tasted bitter in his mouth. This was not who he was, really, but honestly—one had to ensure that the rabble remembered who they were, and who he was. "Can I help you?"

The footman hesitated. "It is just...I am sorry to say you are not permitted upstairs."

Robert stared. *Not—not permitted upstairs?*

There must be some mistake. He had been a member since he reached his majority, far longer ago than he would care to admit. He had been a member before Prinny!

Perhaps longer than the whippersnapper behind the counter had even been born.

"Not permitted upstairs?" he repeated coldly.

The footman shuffled his feet. "'Tis not my decision, my lord, I would not be one to tell you where you can—"

"I should think not!" Robert tried to think, his head befuddled by the smoke.

*Not permitted upstairs?*

Downstairs was the Smoking Room, the Cloakroom of course, and a small room where ladies were permitted if absolutely essential. The last time the Welcoming Room had been used, as far as Robert could remember, it had been to accommodate a Lady Rose, who had been seeking her brother to inform him of their father's sudden death.

And even that had needed special permission from the Proctor.

It was upstairs that the majority of the club lay, why Robert had come in the first place. The Dining Room. The Blue Room, where great antiquities arrived from India and Egypt. The Reading Room, where absolute silence had to be enjoyed for all sound was forbidden.

Dear God, the drinks cabinets were up there!

Robert focused his gaze back onto the footman, who once again shuffled his feet. "I think there has been some mistake."

"No mistake, my lord," said the unfortunate footman. "It is just...well, after your visits to the solicitors..."

Robert's blood went cold.

*No. Surely not.* He had been careful, very careful, to ensure only a very few select people knew about…about Isabelle. Their divorce. In truth, few knew about his marriage at all.

*The judge, a few members of the House of Lords…*Robert tried desperately to rattle through them, eager to uncover who could have revealed the disgrace of his divorce to his club.

Were a few of the lords members here? It was possible. But they were under oath, strict orders not to reveal the goings-on of the chambers elsewhere. What had happened?

"I am sorry, my lord, but we simply cannot permit—"

"Swindmore! I did not know you were a member, too!"

Robert turned around at the unfamiliar voice. What was going to happen next?

For a moment, he could not place the man before him. Oh, he was genteel enough, it was clear he was a gentleman, and he seemed perfectly at home, handing over his coat and top hat to the footman who appeared wordlessly from the cloakroom.

Only when he grinned, a lopsided, easy smile, was Robert able to place him.

Coral de Petras's husband. Edward, if he recalled—did Emerald say he was a duke?

"You have the advantage of me, Your Grace," said Robert formally.

Edward grinned. "It appears I do. Duke of Glaenarm. I must say it is pleasant to see you. Going up?"

Robert caught the eye of the footman behind the counter.

*Ah, a tricky one.* It appeared he had been forbidden the hallowed staircase, and in all other circumstances, he was sure the footman would have ensured it—but with a duke here, and clearly one who knew the marquess…

"I believe I will have to be your guest, Glaenarm," Robert said smoothly, turning back to Edward. "Some sort of mix-up, I'm afraid, I'm being forbidden entrance."

The duke snorted. "Nonsense, we can't have that. Up we go."

Robert walked up the heavy velvet blue staircase with a strange knot in his stomach. This was not the relaxing visit he had come to expect from the Dulverton Club, and now he was in the company of a duke—one with a familial connection to Emerald—he was not quite sure what the afternoon would offer.

It was only as they stepped along the West Corridor and entered the Sun Room—west facing, perfect for drinking as one gazed out on the rooftops of London—did it occur to Robert just precisely how he could take advantage of this rather strange situation.

Why, pump the man for information, of course.

Robert glanced at the duke as they sat in two comfortable chairs by a window. Yes, the duke had been a member of the family a year now, had he not? He would know them all, far better than he did. He would know about Emerald. What made her so delectable as a person, just waiting to be plucked.

*"You want to kiss me, that's all."*

*"I will never ask you to kiss me."*

*"Well, you know your own mind best, I am sure. I just think that one day…you will."*

Robert's stomach lurched. He should leave well enough alone. He'd vowed no entanglements.

You could not find a more ideal woman to seduce if you tried.

Someone cleared their throat. Robert looked up hastily to see a footman. It appeared Edward had given his order, and the man was now waiting for his own.

"A Bordeaux, if you have it, and a brandy if you do not," said Robert with a brief nod.

Well, it was almost midday, was it not?

His gaze fell on the gentleman beside him. Tall, a strong build, and an expression that suggested no nonsense.

Robert swallowed. He needed to leave Emerald well alone. She had a family around her, a family that cared about her greatly and would not see her harmed—nor bedded. The best thing he could do was keep the topics of conversation to light, pleasant things. Politics, wars, and the like.

"Tell me about Emerald."

Robert almost bit his tongue. Well, it was a disaster. How had the words slipped out? Had he not just told himself he would not be asking about the most beautiful de Petras sister?

Edward's eyebrow rose as their drinks were brought over. A large glass of white wine and a brandy.

"Emerald?" repeated her brother-in-law.

"And Sapphire and Micah," said Robert eagerly. "They are an…unusual family."

His companion did not reply at first. Instead, Edward sipped at his wine, sighed appreciatively, and looked out at the scene before them.

"London," Edward said simply. "Magnificent, isn't it?"

Robert glanced at the window. Yes, he supposed it was. As cities went. He had little time for cities, in truth, was little bothered by the dramatic intrigues of gossip and scandal. Give him good weather and good conversation, wherever they could be found, any day.

"Yes," he said shortly. "Very magnificent."

"Though I do not believe you have spent much time in Town," continued the duke. "Busy elsewhere, I hear. Until recently, of course."

The two men's gazes met, and Robert cursed silently within his head.

*Blast.* So, the blaggard knew about Isabelle, then. Well, it was too much to hope the news would be kept entirely quiet. He had managed to keep it out of the newspapers, for which he supposed he should be grateful, but there was always someone willing to whisper.

Robert's fingers tightened around his brandy glass. *That sniveling solicitor.*

"I do not speak of it, but you know to what I am referring," said Edward delicately.

It took a harsh clearing of his throat before Robert could speak. "Yes."

He feared people would assume they knew everything about him as soon as they heard he was divorced.

His cheeks grew hot, and he took a sip of brandy. As though that would help.

"It is none of my business, and I will not share it with the family," said Edward quietly. "A man's life is his own, and I do not believe that sort of...circumstance should change one's fortunes nor fate. One cannot help the fickleness of others."

Something painful shifted within Robert's chest.

*"One cannot help the fickleness of others."*

Perhaps the truest thing ever spoken.

He smiled weakly. "You surprise me, Your Grace."

"Oh, call me Edward, we don't need any of that formality here," said his companion, waving his hand graciously. "And I will call you Robert, if you have no objection."

Robert shook his head. Well, he had come to the club for solace and calm, and he had been met with rudeness and a surprising amount of patience. Not what he had expected.

"So, you are the newest family member," he said delicately.

"Yes, I am—we are an unusual family," said Edward with a laugh. "Our daughters will be de Petrases, though our sons will take my name—which I know would have upset my father greatly if he had been alive to see it. Perhaps that was why I found it so easy."

Robert chuckled and the strange tension between them dissolved.

"I would not have them any other way, you know," Edward continued. "The de Petrases, I mean. They are precisely the sort of people I like. Unaffected, direct, outrageous at times. I imagine you have found them to be such."

"I have indeed," said Robert wryly, thinking of both the Miss de Petrases. No one could accuse Emerald and Sapphire of being placid. "Tell me...tell me about Emerald."

He had been too direct. As Edward took another sip of his wine, Robert tried to remind himself that the last thing he needed was for the family to think he had any sort of…intentions.

Why, it had been clear Opal's expectations were raised when at Almack's. He should have avoided Emerald like the plague since that moment, but for some reason, he was drawn back, inexplicably and yet wonderfully. It may have something to do with that kiss…

Robert's fingers clenched his brandy glass as the memory of that heady kiss rushed through him. He took another sip, the liquid burning his throat but restoring his focus.

"Emerald is a very dear thing," said Edward quietly.

Robert looked up.

The duke laughed under his breath. "Do not think you are the first to ask about her since I married her sister. Emerald de Petras, though she would not care to admit it, is greatly admired by a good number of gentlemen. She dislikes the attention, naturally."

Robert nodded. "If she were anyone else, I would call her a wallflower, but…"

His voice trailed away. But Emerald was so much more than a wallflower, he wanted to say but couldn't. Bolder and braver and brasher. More delicate and more strong. Powerful when she needed to be yet defenseless against the world. She was the most intriguing, most beautiful woman Robert had ever met. Not that he could say that to her brother-in-law…

"I have no wish to be blunt, but I believe I must be."

Robert's head jerked up. Edward was looking at him rather sternly, as a brother would if a gentleman announced the charm of a lady without knowing a family member was present.

He swallowed, his heart skipping a beat. This conversation had got out of hand.

"I warn you," said Edward quietly. "Do nothing."

"Do—"

"Nothing," Edward repeated. "Emerald de Petras has no wish for matrimony and has made her opinion clear on several occasions, though the family themselves…well. Let us say that they have needed a little more convincing. Still, I believe a woman's word should be accepted, and so I warn you. Do not break your heart over Emerald de Petras."

Robert blinked. "Should you not be worried about her heart breaking?"

Edward gave him a lopsided grin. "No, I do not think so. I am still newlywed enough to recognize the signs if you do not mind me saying so. I believe it is your heart in danger of breaking, not hers, to tell the truth."

It was all Robert could do to maintain his composure. Why, if the damned man was not speaking the absolute truth, he would call him out. Most inconvenient it was, that the duke had entirely seen through him.

Conflict rose up in Robert's heart as he took another sip of his brandy and tried to muddle through his ever-changing thoughts.

Yes, Emerald had been clear enough with him when they had first met. She had no wish to dance or converse with gentlemen, no matter their titles. She had been steadfast in that opinion and had only once danced with him at all—and he'd kept his eyes shut. Her kisses…

Robert shuffled uneasily in his seat. Those kisses, warm, passionate, and Emerald had desired such ardor. If anything, he was the one who had been forced to return her home. They could have spent hours there, indulging in each other, luxuriating in the way they—

"Robert?"

Robert started. Edward was looking at him with concern. "Are you quite well?"

"Very well," Robert lied automatically.

Well, he could hardly admit he had been lost in memories of kissing Emerald senseless, could he?

That was the trouble with the woman. Wallflower and heartbreaker. Timid and forceful. Absolutely determined and yet unsure of herself at every quarter.

Robert swallowed as desire rose within him. He was not

going to admit to anything, particularly not to her brother-in-law. He had no wish for matrimony, and neither did she—but then what did that kissing mean? Would he ever tempt her to ask for it again?

*"I will never ask you to kiss me."*

*"Well, you know your own mind best, I am sure. I just think that one day…you will."*

"S-So tell me," said Robert, draining his brandy glass as though that would explain it. "Tell me about the family. An interesting past, I think."

Edward chuckled, shaking his head ruefully. "Oh, you don't know the half of it—and I say that advisedly. I am not entirely sure whether I know the half of it, in truth."

Robert leaned forward. "Really? But you are married to the eldest daughter? I suppose when Micah inherits—"

"No, Coral is the heir."

He must have misheard the man. Robert shook his head, as though there was water in his ears. "I beg your pardon, I thought for a minute there you said—"

"Coral is the heir," repeated Edward, and the jesting smile was gone now. "I tell you, Swindmore," and Robert noted the use of his title, "the family is…complicated. Complicated, and wonderful, and I will protect them to my last breath."

Robert could see that. The de Petrases sparked a strange sort of loyalty, that was clear, and it was a fool who got into the middle of that. *So, was he a fool?*

Edward sighed. "Goodness, I've made a hash of this." He drained his own glass, then leaned forward to look directly into Robert's eyes.

Robert swallowed, his heart pattering painfully.

"The de Petrases," said Edward quietly, "are a family like no other. They will defend their own until the last, even those who do not get on—even Micah."

Robert nodded. Well, it was not unlike many other families he knew, was it?

"I can see you thinking they are not unlike most families, and you would be wrong," Edward said with a dry laugh. "They are more complicated than you know, and unless you really care for her—*really* care, Swindmore, and intend to do something about it...do not get involved. I say it again, leave Emerald de Petras alone."

Robert swallowed. *Care for her—really care.*

Whatever was rushing through his bones whenever he was with Emerald, he could not name—but it was deep. Deeper than anything he had ever known.

"Right," he said aloud, hoping this time his voice sounded stronger. "I will bear that in mind. If I have found myself overcome with a desire to propose to her."

# CHAPTER ELEVEN

*May 24, 1810*

*T**HE SIXTH BALL.*

For the first time since Emerald could remember, she was excited to attend a ball.

"Ems, wait!"

But she did not heed her sister Sapphire's words. Striding into the ballroom, Emerald looked around eagerly for the welcoming face of Robert Ainsworth. Ever since their last meeting, days ago, what felt like a lifetime, she had not stopped thinking about him. About his last words to her.

*"I will never ask you to kiss me."*

*"Well, you know your own mind best, I am sure. I just think that one day…you will."*

Not that she would admit it. Emerald knew her family was confused, bewildered even, by her behavior this evening. Her eagerness to get into the carriage, her demand Sapphire not hold them up, her frustration the carriage was forced to wait more than a minute before depositing them outside.

Emerald swallowed, her gaze flickering across the faces of so many people she did not know.

But no sign of the one gentleman who was able to get her pulse racing, who made Emerald feel…everything. How she had managed to get through days without him—

"What on earth is the rush?"

Emerald turned to smile weakly at her sister. "Rush?"

Sapphire pushed back a lock of hair escaping one of her pins and frowned. "You know precisely what I mean, Ems, so do not try to pretend all innocence with me. Did you have a meeting planned—an assignation?"

Heat seared Emerald's cheeks at the mere mention of something so scandalous. *An assignation?* She had never heard anything so ridiculous in her entire life!

*Except, I could have arranged something with Robert.* He was, after all, most handsome…

*And most unsuitable.* Besides, she had no plans to marry!

"You do confuse me, you know."

Emerald blinked. Sapphire was still frowning, though most of her irritation seemed to have disappeared. "Me? I confuse you?"

She had never met a more confusing, more contrary person in her life as Sapphire de Petras. The idea that she was the confusing one was…well. Confusing.

Sapphire nodded. "Here's Mama, having to force you into a compromise merely to attend ten balls—and I can tell you now, she is not going to count Almack's—"

"I went!"

"You spent less than five minutes in the place, and you know it," shot back Sapphire, though she managed to speak while smiling and fluttering her fan.

Emerald swallowed and looked around them. She must not forget they were in public. Absolutely anyone could be here. They were not sniping at each other in the drawing room at home. They could be overheard.

A rush of panic overwhelmed her.

No one was listening to them.

"I still think it counts," Emerald said quietly, stepping closer to her sister. "Mama gave no precise time that I had to spend at each ball to—"

"You are preposterous, you do know that?" said her sister conversationally.

Emerald could not help but smile. "I do, Sapphy. I really do."

She was being preposterous. Robert had made it perfectly clear what he wanted—at least, when Emerald had got home and tried to think about it, she was almost sure.

He wanted to…well. Kiss her. More than kiss her.

Heat spread across her chest, and Emerald had to hope any onlookers would assume it was the heat of the place causing such a crimson. It was warm. Public balls were always packed, everyone and his mother securing a place, and still more people poured through the doors.

But not him.

Emerald hated she was so eager to see him. Never before had a gentleman taken so much of her…well. Equanimity.

Every day without him felt an age, a punishment, even, for refusing to let him kiss her. Not that she would have let him! A marquess kissing her in Hyde Park! She would never have heard the end of it!

The scandal would have forced him to marry her.

Why did her heart flicker at such a thought?

"Well, something is up."

"Nothing is—"

"You can lie to me all you want," said Sapphire succinctly. "That does not make it true. I am going to find James."

"Sapphy wait, no—"

But Emerald was roundly ignored. It appeared Sapphire had had enough of her sister's mysterious eagerness to be at a ball. She could not blame her. It was quite a departure from her character, Emerald knew, and she would be forced to answer questions in the morning.

Until then…

Stepping to the side to find sanctuary by a wall, Emerald watched the dancers. They appeared to be having a marvelous time and a wistful sense overcame her.

*Dancing.* It did look enjoyable, at least, people seemed to like it. If only she could do it without anyone watching…

The memory of Robert attempting to dance with his eyes closed flashed through her mind, and a strange warmth spread across Emerald's body.

"—surprised to see Swindmore in Town at all."

Emerald froze. *Swindmore?*

Perhaps she had imagined it. As a name, it could easily sound like so many others, after all. Swindley. Swindham. Swinbury. She had been thinking of him, and so—

"Swindmore was a fool to do it in the first place, if you ask me," came another voice.

They were speaking low but were only a few feet before her. Two ladies, speaking behind their fans, evidently not expecting anyone to be behind them. To overhear them.

Emerald's breath caught in her throat. She should move; it was most unseemly of her to remain, now she could hear a private conversation. It would be most uncouth of her to stay.

But stay she did. Gossip about Robert—the Marquess of Swindmore? Unless there was another Swindmore, a cousin perhaps? Heart racing, she willed them to continue, and after a moment the two ladies obliged.

"I think he was bewitched," said the first with a wry laugh. "I mean, Isabelle always had a way with the men!"

"A way that continues, as I hear," replied the second, shaking her head. "Really, the marquess should have known better."

"Men never do."

"You never said a truer word, Mrs. Howarth," nodded her companion.

Emerald knew she needed to breathe. They were talking about Robert—there could be no mistake. Robert, and…and a woman called Isabelle.

A gentleman like that did not kiss like that unless he'd had practice. This Isabelle, whoever she was, must have been his lover. There was no other explanation.

A myriad of emotions rushed through her: panic, confusion, but most of all, curiosity.

A lover of Robert's. Though Emerald was embarrassed to have learned of such a woman from such a gossipy quarter, she was intrigued. What was this Isabelle like? Was she pretty—beautiful, surely. Robert was a handsome man.

Did she let him kiss her, as Emerald had done? More, had they...

Emerald was an innocent, yes, but she was not ignorant. Lovemaking was a fact of nature, a fact of marriage...in some cases, she knew, a fact of life before marriage.

So, Robert had bedded this Isabelle. That, surely, was what this Mrs. Howarth and her friend were talking about.

It was a strange thought. Emerald had known, the moment she had declared to her family that she would never marry—at Coral and Edward's wedding, which now she thought about it was injudicious—that her refusal to take a husband would result in no...experience.

She would never know what it was to be loved, in that way. To be touched in that way. To know pleasure, to know the ecstasy of—

"If you ask me, he made a lucky escape," continued Mrs. Howarth.

Her companion nodded. "To think, if he had not managed to—"

"There you are."

Emerald whirled around, heart beating wildly. There stood Robert, behind her. Had he heard what she had heard—did he know what she now knew?

Embarrassment poured through, boiling her from the inside out. Oh, the shame of being discovered listening to the gossip about another!

"Emerald?" said Robert quietly, stepping closer to her, so close he could almost whisper in her ear. "Are you quite well?"

*Quite well?* Emerald was sure she'd never be well again. She'd overheard snippets of his love affair with another woman, and now she knew he would never wait for her.

Why, there must be countless ladies about the place who would be delighted to receive the attentions of the Marquess of Swindmore. This Isabelle certainly had, anyway.

"If I did not know any better," Robert said slowly, "I would say you were embarrassed. Why are you embarrassed, Emerald?"

"No, I'm not," she said swiftly.

A little too swiftly. His eyes narrowed, a smile dancing upon his lips. "Emerald."

"I-I always look like this," Emerald attempted to bluster. Well, it was almost true, wasn't it? "You have seen me enough at balls, you know how easily my cheeks color."

Robert's gaze flickered from her eyes to her cheeks to her décolletage. Emerald tried not to notice it, the way he appreciated her figure, the way his admiration stirred something deep within her.

It was just a look. A look from a gentleman who made her want to—

"You do not always look like this," said Robert gently. "I know you, Emerald. Perhaps better than you give me credit for."

His gaze moved to her lips once more, and Emerald almost whimpered at the tension between them. He was thinking of their kisses, she knew it—and now she was thinking of it, and longed to find herself in his arms once more, longed to know the heady sensuality of—

But she would not ask him. She would not.

"This is not just embarrassment," Robert said quietly. "This is shame."

Emerald swallowed. What was she meant to do? It would be heartily wrong of her to admit that she enjoyed overhearing gossip about it—more, that she had lapped it up eagerly—yet he was right. She did feel ashamed, and if she knew Robert, he would not cease his questions until he received a sufficient answer.

"Isabelle," she blurted.

The change in him was instantaneous.

Emerald watched, transfixed, as Robert's dark eyes became darker still, a rich, angry, fierce darkness she had never seen before.

His whole demeanor changed. His shoulders grew tight, his jaw tensed, something pulsed in his temple, and Emerald could feel the anger radiating from him, as though something had lit him on fire inside.

To think the mere mention of his paramour's name could enact such a change.

When Robert did speak, it was low under the joyful chatter of the ball, and Emerald had to lean closer to hear him. "What did you say?"

Emerald hesitated, but there was no escaping it, not now. She had spoken a name that evidently brought him a great amount of pain.

And desire.

"I overheard…I mean, I could not help it," Emerald said, sighing as her shoulders slumped. "I suppose I could have helped it, but I did not wish to."

Robert's eyes flared. "Overheard?"

She nodded miserably. There had been trust between them, something special and precious, and now she had ruined it.

"There were two ladies speaking about you and—and a woman called Isabelle. Your lover, I suppose. They said that you were…well. Enamored with her."

Emerald could barely bring herself to watch Robert but she had to. A strange sort of envy, or jealousy, she was not sure which, had overcome her the moment she had seen the effect Isabelle's name had on the man before her.

And she wanted that. She wanted to have that effect, to change the way he stood, his very breathing.

Robert sighed. Raising a hand to his head, he rubbed his eyes for a moment before saying, "Isabelle. Dear God, I never thought

I would hear her name on your lips."

And it was worse, far worse to hear her name on his. Emerald could feel it, the agony of hearing another woman's name from Robert's mouth, and a sense of desperate possessiveness overcame her. She wanted to be the only one he ever spoke of.

"Tell me about her."

The crush in the place was only ever-increasing, the noise of the dancers and the musicians almost overwhelmed by the chatter around them.

Robert did not look away as he spoke. "I do not think you want to hear about—"

"Yes, I do," said Emerald. Somehow, she had taken his hand, and realizing just what that could look like in the eyes of another, she placed her hand on his arm. "Please, Robert."

Whether it was the physical touch or the use of his name, she did not know. Perhaps he could feel the tension in her, the desire, the mixture of hurt and confusion and the sense that she should certainly not be offended that Robert had once kissed another.

"Isabelle was…a woman. Just a woman," Robert said with a heavy sigh. "A woman I was…let us call it, involved with."

Emerald's stomach twisted. So, he had bedded her. Isabelle was his mistress—or had been. Were they still…

"But I am not anymore. Involved, I mean."

A rush of joy soared through her, and Emerald tried not to think about why it mattered so much. But it did. Oh, it did. To know that Robert was hers, and hers alone—

Emerald caught herself. *He was not hers.* She did not own him, and never would. Not if she stuck to her convictions. Convictions that had been put in place long before she had ever crossed the Marquess of Swindmore's path.

Was that his pulse, under her fingertips on his arm, or her own?

"You look disappointed."

"I do?" Emerald tried to smile. "I am not sure what I expected, to be honest. I know that gentlemen have…well, needs, and—"

"Ladies have them, too, you know."

Emerald knew what he meant, knew he meant…well. Love-making. That aching desire that sometimes appeared in the night, after dreams she should not…dreams of him.

"I know," she said, a little too defensively. "My mother once almost took a lover."

Emerald swallowed as her heart skipped a beat, Robert's eyes widening.

Oh, she certainly should not have said that. That was something her mother had told her in confidence, and she could not imagine Opal would ever want that out in the public!

But Robert was not the public. He was Robert. Emerald knew he would not tell a soul.

He certainly looked as though he could hardly believe her words. "I beg your pardon?"

Emerald smiled weakly as they were pushed closer together by the shifting crowd. "You must not tell anyone I—"

"No one would believe me," Robert said. "Goodness, I never would have believed it of your mother, though I suppose you can never tell—"

"It wasn't like that," Emerald said hurriedly.

Oh, she was telling it all wrong, and her mother would be livid!

Panic shifted in her shoulders, tensing her neck and causing a shot of pain to spark into her head. Emerald swallowed. She should never have said—

"It's quite all right."

She looked at him. He was smiling, and it was not a teasing smile, a mischievous one, one she had seen before.

This was…kinder. Softer. The sort of reassuring smile one wished for in a friend.

At least, that was what Emerald had to believe. She had never managed to maintain a friendship with anyone, her shyness overcoming all attempts by well-meaning parties. No, she'd had

Coral and Sapphire, and at times, Micah. James, too, sometimes. Maltravers.

"It was when my father went missing. Misplaced, my mother called it, but as I said before, after seven years he was declared dead," said Emerald quietly. "I mentioned it before."

It felt strange to say these words aloud. They were family issues, after all, and Emerald had found herself mortified whenever she was around anyone who knew the whole truth.

Lady Romeril was the worst.

But saying it all to Robert…well, it did not feel that way. It felt quite the opposite. As though pouring out her heart to him was precisely what she should be doing at a ball.

"And so, Mama was lonely and…well. Had needs," Emerald said, her cheeks slightly pinking. "As you said. Needs she had to…solve."

Well, it was never pleasant to think about one's parents like that.

"And did she?" asked Robert, his eyes even wider.

Emerald had to laugh. "No. The way she tells it, the instant she had decided on a particular gentleman who would suit, Papa stormed into the house, declaring loudly that he was alive, damnit, and he wouldn't have his woman—"

"No!"

"Oh, yes," said Emerald. "And, of course, Papa then had to woo Mama again, as they were not legally married—"

"What?"

In a way, she almost enjoyed this. Being able to shock Robert was not something Emerald thought she could ever do, but seeing him there, utterly astonished, was rather pleasing.

"I said before," Emerald chuckled, "my family are a little…odd."

Robert was nodding. "Yes, I see now what Edward meant."

*Edward?*

Emerald started. Edward? What was Robert doing, talking to her brother-in-law? Talking about her?

She pushed the foolish thought away immediately. Had she not been clear with Robert from the start? There was no possibility he would be talking to anyone about her in that way.

A screaming laugh—the laughter of many. Emerald looked over and saw Sapphire in the middle of a crowd of men, laughing her head off.

"There is always gossip about the de Petras family, and if my siblings have anything to do with it, there always will be," Emerald said wryly.

Robert looked in the same direction and chuckled. "There's no harm in her."

"It harms me." Emerald had spoken in a whisper, hardly sure how she was able to reveal this. "The gossip, the stares, the pointing…all of it. I hate it."

A hand, warm and strong. She looked to see Robert had placed his hand upon hers.

"I did not seek out your brother-in-law for gossip," he said quietly, holding her gaze. "I…I asked him about you."

A deep flush tinged Emerald's cheeks. "Why?"

Robert smiled, his gaze once again flickering to her lips, and Emerald knew in that moment precisely why. "Do I need to explain it?"

# CHAPTER TWELVE

*June 1, 1810*

*T*HE SEVENTH BALL.

There was something about a ball in June.

But a ball in June, particularly one like this…well, he had never known Lady Romeril's garden to look so stunning. The lamps her servants had positioned about the place gave a lovely warm glow to the early evening, the sun hanging lazily on the horizon as the candles flickered in the gentle breeze.

He had almost declined the invitation.

Well, Lady Romeril was—at least, *Lord* Romeril had been relatively low status, for a gentleman with a title. Nothing impressive at all, and the Swindmore title had been handed down…what. *Fifteen generations?*

But then a snippet of a memory seared into his mind, and Robert had almost blotted his ink across his note.

*"My sister's godmother, Lady Romeril, does not take kindly to such words."*

Sapphire de Petras's godmother. He was not misremembering, was he?

It did not seem likely. Everything Emerald said and did was indelibly marked on his mind, and he was certain she had spat at that brigand of a gentleman that her younger sister had Lady

Romeril as a godmother.

That had to mean the de Petrases would be invited, would it not?

Robert felt nothing but disappointment as he meandered through the gardens, set out by Capability Brown, he overheard someone mutter in dry praise, seeing nothing of the green-eyed woman he had hoped to see here.

"Ah, Swindmore."

Turning, Robert found for a moment that he could not place the beaming gentleman striding toward him who had evidently said his name.

A tall chap with a cheerful smile and a sense of familiarity Robert was unaccustomed to. Well, it was not as though he had much of an acquaintance in London.

"Maltravers," said the gentleman when he reached him, bowing. "Friend of the de Petras family, we met at—"

"Ah, yes, I remember now," said Robert hastily. "How are you?"

He bowed his head in polite reply as the younger gentleman rattled on about races and horses and some sort of bet he'd put on with Micah de Petras, but Robert struggled to pay attention.

His gaze darted behind the chattering man. Surely, they would be here?

"They're over there."

Robert started. The Earl of Maltravers's smile had twisted into something rather knowing, as though there was a kinship between them Robert had not yet recognized.

"I beg your pardon?" he tried to ask loftily.

Maltravers's smile broadened. "Do not worry, I have seen that face before—in my own mirror, in fact."

The man sounded a little wistful, and Robert could not understand it. Seen that face before? What was the man talking about?

"There, I tell you," said the man, pointing over Robert's shoulder with a dry laugh. "You missed them because of that large shrub, I do not know what Lady Romeril was thinking, letting her son redesign this part of the garden…"

Maltravers continued to talk, but Robert did not hear him, other than registering his words as vague chatter underneath the growing noise of the ball. That was because he had turned around in the direction that the man was pointing and seen something rather remarkable.

*Emerald.* Emerald, standing in a light green dress with elegant, pleated ruffles around her bodice that highlighted just how lithe her figure was. Her hands clasped together, as always, unadorned with jewels.

Robert's stomach lurched. *She needed none.* A simple pearl choker around her neck with a small emerald pendant was all she needed, and even then, she shone brighter than any of them.

She stood with her family, but they paled into insignificance as Emerald caught his eye and smiled.

And that was it. She had turned and seen him, and Robert was entirely in her power. There was nothing he would not do for her. Nothing.

For in that smile, he saw so many unexpressed words. Pleasure to see him, reassurance there was someone there she knew. A delight in his presence that made Robert want to stride over, pull Emerald from her family, and kiss her senseless.

She was stunning. He certainly felt stunned. Robert tried to shake his head, without anyone noticing. There appeared to be cotton wool stopped up in his ears; for a moment, all sound at the ball had disappeared.

"My lord?"

Maltravers had spoken—at least, Robert assumed it was Maltravers. It was not Emerald, so it did not matter.

Robert took a hesitant step toward her, and her smile widened.

His heart skipped a beat. She was happy to see him; something small or inconsequential with any other woman, but for Emerald, it was praise of the highest degree.

Who else did she smile for? No one, as far as Robert could see, and he wanted to keep it that way. Wanted to keep all her glorious joy for himself.

*Oh, damn.*

He cared for her. Despite all his precautions, despite telling himself—and her—that he had no interest in anything more serious than a stolen kiss, Robert had to admit, as he took another shaky step toward her, that Emerald was fast becoming his only reason for being.

Panic fluttered at the edges of his heart. He had never intended for his heart to become tangled with another—but this felt different. Isabelle had wanted him for the power of his position, the prestige, her ability to take what she wanted and leave.

And leave she had.

But Emerald was not like that. In truth, Robert was not entirely sure whether Emerald knew she had fallen in love with him yet.

After all, he had only just discovered it himself.

Emerald's smile broadened, and Robert tried not to puff his chest out with pride.

*He had done it.* He had captured something intensely precious, the good graces of Emerald de Petras. But did she know it? Did she understand this hot, senseless feeling within her, as he did…as love?

"Miss de Petras," Robert said formally, bowing.

Emerald replied with a curtsey but said nothing, her green eyes bright as they met his.

"Ah, your lordship, I hoped we would run into you," said Opal de Petras loudly.

Robert glanced round and saw Lady Romeril watching them closely. *Blast.* The woman was a worse gossip than most of London put together—but surely, she would do nothing to harm her friend and her daughters?

The matriarch of the de Petras family seemingly had not finished. "I was just saying to Emerald the other day, I wondered when you could come to call and—"

"Miss de Petras," said Robert, speaking over her, all eyes for Emerald. "I wondered whether you would honor me with a walk around the gardens."

Both Sapphire and Jasper de Petras looked at Emerald.

Robert found he was holding his breath. This was madness; he had no reason to believe Emerald would not grace him with such a treat. Even if her family were watching on.

But she hesitated. Her gaze flickered to her family, then returned to him, and a heat Robert had never felt before rushed through his veins at her considered look.

Oh, if only he could get her away from these people, in a darkened corner, behind a tree…

Robert grinned. "It's either a walk or dancing."

Sapphire giggled and was firmly nudged by her father, though this did not cease her laughter. Robert winked, exultation flowing through him, and she giggled again.

"A walk," Emerald repeated.

Robert luxuriated in the sound of her voice. The moment he got her away, he wanted to hear her speak. All her thoughts and opinions. All that others ignored because she was shy.

"A walk," he said quietly, offering his arm.

"Emerald, dear, I really think you should dance with other gentle—"

"Thank you, Mama, for your opinion," Emerald cut across her mother. "But I have made my choice."

*I have made my choice.*

It was difficult not to feel like the king of the world as Emerald took his arm. Robert swallowed, knowing his instinct to speak must be ignored, and merely bowed his head at the rest of the de Petras family—noting Jasper's grin and Opal's look of astonishment—before he and Emerald started to walk along the grassy path.

"You should not have been so bold," came Emerald's gentle words.

Robert grinned. Well, how could he not? He had the most beautiful woman at Lady Romeril's ball on his arm, he had managed to whisk her away from her family with very little trouble—and thankfully, no suggestion of scandal—and he had a plan…

"Bold? You call me bold, after speaking to your mother like that?"

A smile parted Emerald's lips. "Boldness is not something I am usually accused of."

"No, I suppose not," said Robert. "And yet…"

His voice trailed away. What he had been about to say was not appropriate; at least, it was not the elegant flirting she had surely come to expect.

Oh no, it was far more heartfelt. Too heartfelt, perhaps.

"Yet?"

Robert glanced at the woman on his arm. She was smiling still, her eyes bright, her whole body leaning into him. As though she trusted him. As though she truly cared for him.

He swallowed. He would have to be careful here; it was rather akin to playing with fire, but with flames that had a life of their own.

"Yet I like you as you are," he said simply, deciding against self-censorship. She had a right to know, did she not, how he felt? "Wallflower, shy, nervous, whatever you want to call it. I like you as you are."

Emerald's eyes had widened, and the smile had disappeared. Robert cursed himself for being so forward, so inelegant. What woman wanted to hear that?

"A-As I am?"

Robert nodded. "Yes."

They passed a gaggle of people pouring down a path that led to a rose garden. Walking in silence, Robert steered them along a quieter path.

"I do not think anyone has ever said that to me before."

Emerald's voice was quiet, brimming with emotion, and

Robert cursed himself once again. How was it possible that he wished to say so much, yet managed to say so little?

"How…how is the agreement going?" That was it, change the subject. Anything to avoid his own foolish feelings that he had in no way managed to articulate.

And perhaps that was for the best.

Emerald took a deep breath, as though she recognized his desire to begin the conversation again. "Agreement? You mean my compromise with my mother, the ten balls?"

Robert nodded as they turned a corner. Musicians started up somewhere, a very elegant tune, but it was getting quieter and quieter with every step.

"Well, this is the seventh ball, and I think the one I have best liked so far," admitted Emerald. "There is something about having a ball outside in a garden, do not you think?"

Seventh ball. He could hardly believe they had gone by so fast. *Seventh? That meant…*

"So, it is almost over then?" He could not help disappointment seeping into his voice.

The evening was starting to grow dark now. The sun had just dipped completely under the horizon, birds singing their last lament to the day before they disappeared off to sleep. Night was approaching.

Emerald squeezed his arm, and Robert looked into her eyes as she spoke softly. "You know, balls are not the only place where one can meet with a…a friend. If you wanted to—I mean," she added, seeming to catch herself in a scandalous suggestion, "if you wanted to, there is no expectation that you should…"

Her voice chattered away, and Robert could hear the tension, the panic she had spoken out of turn, but his heart leapt at her words.

She wished to see more of him—beyond meeting at balls. She must care for him; it could not all be his imagination. He could not be dreaming the brightness of her eyes, the way she leaned into him as they walked, her silence now they were in the depths of Lady Romeril's garden, away from every other guest.

Alone.

"I-I…" Robert swallowed. He was not going to lose his head! "I think I would be fortunate to see you at any time, in any place."

He watched as a flush appeared on her cheeks. As Emerald dropped her gaze, Robert stopped her in their tracks. He lifted up her chin with a finger, captured her gaze once more, and felt his loins tighten.

Oh, he wanted her—but willingly. He wanted all of her, as much as she would give.

"You are beautiful, you know," Robert whispered.

Emerald's eyes shone with something he could not fathom. "You and your nonsense."

"No! No, you have to believe me," insisted Robert.

How could he make her see? How could she not see whenever she gazed in a looking glass? Was it not there for the world to see? Her gentle elegance, the curve of her lips, the bright, glorious green of her eyes? The way her fingers clasped together, as though desperate for reassurance, the tilt of her head as she laughed…

"Emerald," Robert said quietly, "Emerald, I…I do not know if I have ever fallen in love before…perhaps I thought I did, but I could not—I mean, knowing what I know now…"

Her eyes widened and she did not move away from him. To the contrary, Emerald closed the distance between them, taking his hands in hers. They were warm. Robert could feel her pulse quicken in her fingertips.

His heart raced, matching hers. They were such a match, were they not? A match he could not have fathomed, a match he had never expected to find.

"Now I know," whispered Robert, "that…that I have never been in love."

Emerald's breath caught in her throat. "Robert—"

"Not until I met you."

There. The words were said. Robert could hardly believe it. Had he ever meant them before, really meant them, to his core?

No. Whatever Isabelle had inspired, it was not this, this protective, dark, possessive, worshipful need to be near Emerald with every moment of his existence.

Yet she was silent. Robert looked deep into those green eyes as Emerald stared, mouth open, obviously stunned by his revelation. Could he have said it better? Perhaps he should—

"Kiss me," Emerald breathed.

Robert needed no further invitation. Pulling her into his arms, he bestowed a hungry kiss on her willing and eager lips, almost moaning.

This was where he belonged. This was where he wanted to be. This was everything he wanted. She was everything he desired, and the sweet succulent taste of her hit a spot in his heart Robert had never known was starving.

"Emerald," he murmured, tilting her back to allow him greater access to her mouth.

His tongue met hers, and she quivered in his arms, and Robert could have cried with gratitude. He had her. Emerald de Petras, in his arms. Perhaps soon, in his bed…

Emerald's fingers entwined themselves in his hair, pulling him closer, and Robert did not hold back. His teasing tongue was mirrored by his hands, moving from her waist to her buttocks, pulling her toward him as he ached for more contact.

More, more. He needed more.

And she did not stop him.

Robert looked into her eyes, heavy with lust. "Emerald?"

There was nothing like Emerald, nothing he had ever known, no woman had ever tasted so sweet.

Her chest heaved as her breath quickened, and Robert could not help himself. One of his hands left her buttocks and crept slowly but surely up her bodice, eventually enclosing one breast.

Emerald arched into him and tilted back her head, and there was nothing he could do but be carried along by this swell of passion—and that was not the only thing that was swelling.

Robert tried his best to ignore the throbbing ache in his manhood pressed against Emerald's hips as he lowered his lips to her neck, leaving a trail of kisses to her décolletage.

Emerald...oh, she did something to him, something he could not comprehend and did not want to. As long as the kisses continued...

How long they stood there, panting, murmuring each other's names whenever they had enough breath—and were not kissing—Robert did not know. Not long enough.

A sudden burst of light and noise, and he lifted his head, hating he had broken the connection between them. He saw the reflection of fireworks in Emerald's eyes and his stomach lurched most painfully.

How had he managed to fall in love with a woman who had no desire for matrimony?

Emerald smiled, curling her fingertips down his jawline, brushing them across his lips.

Robert quivered, utterly lost to her charms. He could never say no to her now; he was completely in her power. Not that Emerald would ever ask anything wild of him, of course.

And then she did something Robert could never have predicted.

"I want you to make love to me."

# CHAPTER THIRTEEN

EMERALD STARED UP into the dark eyes of a man she had just…propositioned?

*"I want you to make love to me."*

Her own words rang in her mind, as scandalous in her memory as when first spoken.

She could not have said them. Perhaps she had only thought them, desperate desire welling up within her thanks to Robert's delicious kisses.

But no, he was looking at her as though she had said them, mouth agape, hands still tight around her. Hands she never wanted removed. Hands she wanted all over her body, without the interference of fabric or the possibility that they could be discovered…

Heat rushed through Emerald at the mere thought. They were standing in Lady Romeril's garden, after all, during a ball. It was perfectly possible someone else could meandcr this way, come across them pressed up against a tree and kissing as though their lives depended on it…

Emerald attempted to catch her breath, but it was impossible. Not with those words now hanging in the air between them.

*"I want you to make love to me."*

How had she found the bravery to say those words?

Perhaps it was not bravery, but foolishness. Emerald would

certainly have labeled anyone else who said those words out loud, to a gentleman, as a foolish woman.

But she had said them—rather, they had poured from her mouth before she had known how to stop them.

Because she wanted him. Wanted all of him, all of her, the two of them, sharing something she knew she would never share with another.

Who else would she find to care for her like Robert? As the cool night air breezed past, Emerald tried not to think too much about the words he had so recently admitted.

*"You are staring at me."*

*"I am indeed."*

*"W-Well I—I wish you wouldn't."*

*"There is no law against looking at a beautiful woman."*

She would never find a gentleman like him, bold and caring, direct yet gentle. Robert was the most handsome man she had ever managed to hold a conversation with.

Emerald almost laughed. Not that that was saying very much.

But he cared. Had he not said he loved her?

*"Now I know that...that I have never been in love. Not until I met you."*

Emerald had never imagined anyone would say those words to her. At least, not like this. Family yes, but they loved her because they had to. Because that was right. Because that was what one did.

But Robert? He loved her with passion, a passion she could still taste on her lips. He loved her not ignoring her faults and foibles, but in some way, because of them. And he desired her. Pressed up against him as she was, Emerald could still feel the bulge in his breeches, and though she was an innocent, she was no fool.

He wanted her, as much—perhaps more—than she did. All he had to do was give in.

"I-I beg your pardon?" breathed Robert.

Emerald managed a half smile as she repeated her words. "I

want you to make love to me."

He was staring as though she was speaking a foreign language, but to Emerald, it was quite simple.

She was never going to be married. That was not going to change. It was a decision she had made long ago, and she still saw no reason to change it now. He said he loved her, but there was no proposal, no offer of marriage. She knew well enough that he agreed with her; marriage was a mistake, one neither of them wished to make.

A shiver rushed down her spine, but Emerald pushed it aside. If she was to remain unmarried, as she intended, that would mean a complete ignorance of such delicious things as she could share with Robert, tonight.

Emerald swallowed. Robert had not proposed matrimony; it was clearly not on his mind. Why, if he had such honorable intentions, would he not have asked to speak to her father this evening, instead of taking her on this evidently planned secret assignation in the dark?

Another firework went off in the distance, and she heard a number of gasps from Lady Romeril's guests. They seemed very far away.

"I...I do not..." Robert cleared his throat, not letting go of Emerald as he coughed. "Emerald, you do not know what you are talking about."

Emerald raised an eyebrow as boldly as she could manage. "Don't I?"

She leaned forward, hardly able to believe what she was doing, and kissed Robert gently on the neck. Then not so gently.

A low moan uttered from his throat as she felt him melt into her arms.

"I know what I want," she murmured as Robert clutched her tightly. "And I know what I want from you. Just one night...just to know what it's like..."

"Emerald," groaned Robert, and then, sharper, "Emerald!"

He stepped back, leaving Emerald to lean against the tree and look at him, glorying in this wild conversation. Had she ever spoken of such things—desire, lust, pleasure?

"Emerald de Petras, you entirely confuse me," said Robert, a wry smile on his face as he shook his head. "I say that I love you, and you—you say you want me to bed you?"

Heat scalded her cheeks. "When you put it like that—"

"I did not say I was complaining," Robert interjected, taking her hand in his.

Emerald looked at their intertwined fingers. She rather liked seeing them, a sense that they were bound together. Bound closer than anyone she ever had been.

"I just want you to be sure."

She looked up, another firework sparkling in the distance, light shimmering in his eyes. Sure? She had never been more sure of anything in her entire life. The more she thought about it, the more perfect it was.

"I am sure."

It was not fireworks that lit up Robert's eyes this time, but something within, something deeper, something darker. Something Emerald had never seen before.

Something she wanted to see again.

Robert grinned. "Come on then."

Before Emerald could reply, he had launched forward, pulling her behind him. Her heart pattered strangely yet there was no discomfort in her stomach, no signs she had made an awful mistake. No, there was naught but excitement. *Where was he taking her?*

The sounds of the ball, musicians, laughter, the stamping of feet on a makeshift dancefloor, and the gentle tinkle of glass washed over them as they crept through the garden onto the street.

It was absolutely rammed with carriages, and Emerald had no breath to say a word as Robert pulled her along and stopped outside a carriage with a red crest.

"After you," he said quietly.

Emerald glanced around. There was no one else on the street, save for the coachmen sitting, waiting for their masters and mistresses to return. No one to see them, no one who would know she had crept into the Marquess of Swindmore's coach.

His driver started, dozing with the horses' reins in his hands. "M'lord?"

"Home," muttered Robert as he opened the door.

Emerald hesitated only a moment. Once she stepped into that carriage, there was no knowing what was going to happen—at least, there was a certainty of what would happen, and it was scandalous. Certainly something she should not be doing.

"Emerald?"

She took a deep breath and stepped into the carriage.

Robert followed her immediately, and before she could say a word, Emerald found herself pulled into his arms, his lips on hers, and it was everything, the world shaking or perhaps it was the carriage moving forward, she could not tell, for she was wrapt within Robert.

"I'm going to have to try to stop," muttered Robert as he pulled his coat off while still kissing down Emerald's neck.

It was all she could do to cling to the carriage seat and let him kiss her. "Why?"

"Because if I'm not careful," came the delicious reply, "I'll take you right here, right now, in this carriage."

Emerald whimpered. *Take her?* Oh, she wanted him to take her, wanted to know what that pleasure was, wanted to lose herself in his embraces—and her whimper spurred him on.

His waistcoat fell to the floor of the carriage just as it pulled up.

Robert groaned, his head falling onto her shoulder. "We're here," came his whisper.

Emerald blinked. *Here. Where?*

Then it all rushed back to her; yes, they were in a carriage. They had been going somewhere. She had become so entranced with Robert's kisses, with his caresses, she had almost forgotten where they were.

Robert pulled her toward him, through the open door, and Emerald half stepped, half stumbled onto the pavement. The townhouse they were standing outside was tall, at least three stories high, and a shiver rushed up her spine.

Once she stepped over that threshold…

"Emerald?"

It was as though he could feel her uncertainty. Emerald looked up at Robert, the man who had been kissing her senseless in the carriage, and knew—as certainly as one knew right from wrong, hunger from pain, that she wanted to be with him.

She wanted him. She wanted everything he could give her, and would take it.

"Robert," she breathed.

The sound of his name appeared to reassure him. He grinned. "Come inside."

Emerald crossed the threshold into the silent hallway of Robert's home.

She had not known what to expect. It was a bachelor's home, and she had never been inside a man's home before. Micah's rooms did not count; they were merely taken, one bad-tempered afternoon, to hole himself up somewhere that wasn't their parents' home.

Everywhere else Emerald had been—and in truth, she had not accepted many invitations—had been the homes of ladies. That is, ladies with husbands. Lady Romeril's, the Lenskeyns, Lady Stulsemere…

Robert's hallway had a grandfather clock, just like Lady Romeril's, and it had a console table by the door and a coat rack and hat stand, just as her own home did. There was nothing remarkable about it.

"Emerald?"

Emerald blinked. So lost in her thoughts, she had almost forgotten why she was here in the first place, not that her heart had. It still thumped away, and as she met Robert's gaze, it skipped a beat.

She was here to make love to a marquess. What a contrary debutante she would be—if she could be considered a debutante.

"Upstairs," murmured Robert. "All the servants will be abed, and in less than five minutes, that's precisely where I want you."

He was meant to say such things. She would be more mortified if he did not.

The staircase opened up onto a long landing, and Robert pulled her to a door.

Emerald's mouth fell open. This...this could not be his bedchamber.

It was huge. At least three times the size of hers, if not more, the room had heavy long curtains at one end and a magnificent four-poster bed at the other.

A very large bed.

Emerald swallowed, attempting to hide her shock at the intimacy of the room. Was that where...

*"Isabelle was...a woman. Just a woman. A woman I was...let us call it, involved with. But I am not anymore. Involved, I mean."*

She could not think that way. Robert had a past, yes, but did not every gentleman? Why, she would be hard pushed to find a gentleman in the entirety of London, Emerald was sure, who had not a single dalliance under his belt.

"Emerald..."

She sank into the embrace as Robert pulled his arms around her from behind and kissed her neck. Eyelashes fluttering closed, unable to bear the intensity of the connection, she sighed happily as his kisses sparked new longing.

"I want to see you," came Robert's jagged voice.

Emerald gasped as she was whirled around and leaned back as his fingers started to pull at the ties of her gown.

Robert stopped immediately. "We don't have to—"

"I know," Emerald said, cutting across him.

She hardly knew why she had leaned back in the first place; instinct had taken over, and she had known, deep within herself, that she could not permit Robert to look at her.

Oh, he would mean well. He may not even say anything. But the knowledge he had bedded at least one other woman—this Isabelle—had changed something within her heart.

He would compare them.

There was a look of deep confusion on Robert's face, illuminated by a single candle left in his bedchamber for when returning from the ball.

Emerald almost laughed. *The ball! Lady Romeril's ball!* They would have to make up some excuse later.

"I do not understand," said Robert quietly, his eyes never leaving hers. "I thought you wanted—but if you don't—"

"I do," said Emerald wretchedly. Oh, how would she explain! "I don't want you to…"

Her breath was short, part passion, part panic, but Robert did not interrupt her nor speak over her. He stood there, arms by his sides in reverent restraint, and Emerald adored him all the more for it.

He would not rush her. He would not make demands of her she could not fulfill.

He was unlike anyone she had ever met.

Robert smiled genially as Emerald managed to meet his eyes. She could do this. If he decided to laugh…well, then he simply wasn't worth it at all, was he?

Heartened by this thought, Emerald took a deep breath. "I don't want you to look at me while we…we…"

The actual words failed her right at the last, but that did not seem to matter. Robert's eyes had widened with understanding, and Emerald swallowed, hoping he would not censure her for the fear she felt.

"Emerald," said Robert quietly. "Emerald, I will do nothing you do not wish, but you are beautiful."

She had to laugh. *Well, what nonsense!*

"Inside and out," he continued in a low voice, ignoring her scoff. "I want to look at you when I make love to you. If there is anyone in the world who you should let look at you, it's me."

He spoke with such certainty, such sincerity, Emerald hardly knew where to look. He could not be in earnest…yet there was honesty in Robert's eyes, honesty she could not deny.

Emerald did not trust her voice. She nodded.

Excitement flashed in his face, heartfelt and true, and Robert reached for her with hesitancy Emerald recognized more in herself than in him.

Her body trembled as his fingers reached the ties of her gown.

"You are beautiful," said Robert quietly, kissing her cheek as he spoke. "Beautiful not just because of your eyes, which sparkle like jewels, or your smile, which I believe is brighter than the sun."

Emerald shivered as Robert's kisses trailed down her neck, his fingers gently untying her gown. This was too much, far too much, yet she did not want it to stop. She did not want him to stop.

"You are beautiful because of who you are," Robert whispered, lowering her gown.

Emerald swallowed, breath tightening. She was standing in only her chemise and stays! No one had ever seen her like this—except her modiste, and Madame Jacques did not—

"I first saw how beautiful you were when you told me you would not dance with me," murmured Robert, kissing her shoulder as he delicately lifted her chemise from it. "And the second time you refused my hand, and the third—"

"I wondered why you kept asking," Emerald breathed as he kissed her other shoulder, lifting her chemise from it.

The chemise fell to the ground, and something stirred just below her stomach.

"Because I could not stay away from you," replied Robert with a dry laugh, his fingers now gently untying her stays. "Because the moment I realized your true beauty was the very first time I saw you. Before we were introduced. Before I even knew your name."

Emerald's head tilted back as Robert's lips halted speaking, meeting the very tops of her breasts, pleasure rippling through her body.

"Th-The first time?"

Her mind was entirely overtaken with him, with what he was doing to her. Such gentle touches, fiery kisses, words of desire? It was a miracle she was still standing.

Her stays fell to the floor, and Emerald looked shyly at Robert as she stood, naked.

"The very first time," said Robert quietly, a smile dancing across his face. "When you defended your sister. I knew then you were a remarkable and desirable woman."

Emerald gasped—not because of his words, but because of his actions. Before she could say a thing, refute his foolishness, explain that anyone would have defended Sapphy against such miscreants, Robert had lifted her and carried her to the bed, throwing her onto it.

"Robert!"

He did not have time to reply either. Robert was hastily pulling off his clothes, boots, waistcoat, cravat, and shirt all falling in a haze of linen and cotton—and when he straightened up...

Emerald swallowed. Well. That was a man, then.

"Emerald, I have already told you I love you tonight," said Robert with a smile, joining her on the bed and pulling her into him. "And—"

"Robert!" Emerald gasped.

She had been unable to help herself. The intensity of the sensation, his skin against hers, was too much to go unnoticed, unmentioned. Oh, it was sweet agony, her legs entangled with his, her breasts against his chest—

"I want you to know," Robert said, kissing her between every word, and Emerald tried to capture his lips with hers, prolong a kiss, "that I love you. You do know that, don't you?"

"Yes," Emerald moaned.

Something was building inside her. An ache, a glorious, wonderful ache that only Robert could satisfy. Why wasn't he giving her everything—she wanted everything.

"I want you," she gasped.

Robert groaned. "I know you do."

And then he was inside her—actually inside her, and Emerald could hardly believe she had done it, she had made love!

But that did not appear to be all. As Robert leaned against one elbow, his other hand stroking her face, her neck, brushing exquisitely past a nipple before grasping her hip, he thrust into her again, his manhood going deeper this time, and Emerald's whole body focused on where they met, every heartbeat growing the ache, that pleasurable need, and he seemed to know that, seemed to know what she needed.

"More," Emerald moaned.

"Yes, yes," Robert half-whispered, half-groaned as he captured her lips once more.

And then she was on fire. Emerald could hardly contain herself as the overwhelming pleasure soared through her, taking captive every inch of her body, her limbs shaking, her body convulsing with ecstasy.

He fell into her arms. Emerald clutched him, hardly sure how she was breathing, her panting mingling with his own, and she knew, then.

Despite all her efforts, despite all her promises to herself and others...she had not only fallen in love but now wanted to marry Robert Ainsworth, Marquess of Swindmore.

# CHAPTER FOURTEEN

*June 2, 1810*

THERE WAS SOMETHING very different about Robert's bed when he awoke.

It couldn't be the sheets. They had been changed regularly every Wednesday since before Robert could remember.

It wasn't the light. The soft summer light drifted past the curtains and onto his pillow, but it always did this time of year. It was one of the things he liked the best about his room. The warmth drifted in along with the light, helping him to stir from his sleep into vague wakefulness—and usually before ten o'clock in the morning, too.

But there was a different sort of warmth beside him today. Robert did not need to open his eyes to know what it was; had he not lived with a woman for years? Had not Isabelle been careful to make her presence, and her absence, keenly felt?

For a moment, just before he permitted himself to open his eyes and see what sort of mistake he had made last night; he wished to goodness he had been more careful. Had he not promised himself no complications after Isabelle?

Robert opened his eyes.

Beside him, hands underneath her pillow and dark curls of chestnut hair covering most of her face, was Emerald de Petras.

Robert's heart twisted, and all the tension in his stomach melted away.

A smile drifted across Robert's face. *Emerald.* A strange jolt sparked across his chest as a realization hit him.

For the first time in his life, he had awoken with a woman in his bed…and no regrets.

*"I want you."*

*"I know you do."*

Robert could hardly believe it. Swallowing his emotions, he feasted his eyes on the woman beside him. A woman who was still quite clearly naked.

How was it possible that he could live more than thirty years, and never experience this until now? The utter certainty that the woman in bed beside him belonged there?

Emerald shifted in her sleep, and Robert held his breath, as though that would change whether she awoke or not. For a heart-stopping moment, he thought she was waking, and was thrown into a panic.

Emerald settled, sighing gently as she curled her hands tighter around her pillow.

Robert swallowed. Oh, it had been better than he could have imagined—she had been better. Bolder, and yet shyer.

That was the strange and wonderful thing about Emerald. He found he had no desire to change her in any respect from the nervous, uncertain woman that she was. At least, uncertain when it came to herself. When it came to others, she was most definitely sure.

A flicker of amusement fluttered across his heart. Emerald was absolutely perfect just the way she was, though she evidently did not think so.

*"I don't want you to look at me while we…we…"*

*"I want to look at you when I make love to you. If there is anyone in the world who you should let look at you, it's me."*

He had never experienced that before, a connection beyond body, beyond pleasure, though there was certainly enough of it to keep him more than satisfied.

But it had been deeper. With Emerald their joy had met, mingled, their touches exciting each other, her pleasure and joy growing as his did.

What he would do to experience that again…perhaps every night…

Emerald's eyes fluttered open. "Mmm."

It was the soft, gentle sigh of a person slowly waking up and, Robert could quite clearly see, a person who had not yet taken in where they were…or who they were with. He watched as she shifted in his bed, twisting comfortably with a smile on her lips— a smile that froze as she met his gaze.

A rush of scarlet tinged her cheeks. "Robert!"

"That's what they call me."

Why, he could almost laugh if he was not afraid Emerald may misunderstand. This was glorious, was it not? They loved each other! At least, he loved her, and he had to assume a woman of Emerald's breeding and natural shyness would not permit herself to be bedded unless there was some deep emotion there.

*Wouldn't she?*

"Oh, my goodness, I cannot believe—"

"Good morning," said Robert, pulling her into his arms. "And don't worry."

It was rather difficult to prevent desire sparking within him as he felt the softness of Emerald. It was wonderful and painful all at the same time. Painful to think that at any moment, she would be wrenched from his arms. That she would not always be here, in his bed, waiting for him.

That somehow his life would not be able to continue without her…

"Worry?" Emerald sighed, relaxing into his embrace, her hand placed on his chest. "What is there to worry about?"

He almost chuckled. What was there to worry about? Only that they had disappeared together, from Lady Romeril's ball, getting into his carriage, and leaving for the entire night…

Emerald would not have been discovered at home, and if she was not at home…

Only her reputation. Only scandal.

"You know," Robert said, "you are not nearly as concerned as I thought."

Perhaps he should not have spoken.

Emerald stiffened in his embrace. "Concerned?"

Robert swallowed. He had ruined it, all by opening his stupid mouth. All he'd had to do was stay quiet, indulge in the pleasure of this moment, and he'd had to say something.

"Concerned," he repeated. "Yes, I mean…a lady of your reputation, your family…I thought—I assumed—"

"You would probably have presumed right," came the shy voice from just below his chin. "At least, a few weeks ago—maybe a few days ago…I never thought this would happen."

Robert tightened his arms around the woman he cared for. "That makes two of us."

"I am in earnest!"

"So am I!" he protested, smiling at the teasing nature of their conversation. *Oh, if only every morning could begin like this…* "You have to remember, it was not a few months ago that I was desperately requesting your hand for a mere dance. And now—"

"Now you have all of me," came Emerald's gentle voice.

All of her. He had admitted his love for her, affection dripping from his lips, and all Emerald had done was demand that he make love to her.

He would have to hope he'd met her expectations.

"All of you," he breathed.

"And now that it has happened, I-I am glad," said Emerald quietly. She lifted her head and smiled shyly. "I mean—I could not imagine it, and I wanted it, and now it's happened—"

"It was perfect."

Robert had not intended to interrupt her. The words had just flowed through him. She had to know how perfect it had been, how perfect she had been—how perfect she was.

There was a part of his heart belonging to her, irrevocably, and it was impossible to imagine a world without her. A life that did not include Emerald? Not a life worth living.

"Perfect?" Emerald's brow puckered into a frown. "Truly? Y-You say that, after…"

Her voice trailed away, and Robert's stomach churned horribly.

*After Isabelle.* That's what she was going to say, even if she would not. After his wife.

It was a strange thing, to have had a wife and now to be without one—and to be entirely glad of that fact. But it was not just that Isabelle had been no wife to him for many a month before the eventual paperwork rendered that relationship obsolete.

No, it was that with Isabelle by his side, he never would have met Emerald. As though she had been designed for him. As though they had been designed for each other.

Emerald smiled. "But this is different, isn't it?"

Robert's heart swelled. "Yes. Yes, different—more different than you could know."

She lifted her head to be kissed, and he bestowed several very willingly. Oh, she understood him on a deeper level than Robert knew was possible. How did she do it? How could she be a part of him in a way that no one ever had been?

Because this was different. As Emerald settled back into his arms and sighed happily, he came to the realization he would do anything, anything, if it meant having her like this, in his arms, for the rest of his life. And that meant only one thing.

*Matrimony.*

Robert swallowed. Emerald needed to be a part of his life. Propose matrimony and ask her to be his wife.

*"I have no wish to get married."*

That was perhaps the only difficulty. Robert was no fool—he knew full well the de Petras family would be thrilled to receive his addresses for Emerald.

But would she? After all her words on the subject, after her distinct desire not to dance with anyone, after her shyness, her frustration with Society…

Would she, even after all they had shared, be open to becoming his wife?

She must be comfortable here, in his arms, if she was able to drift off to sleep without a care in the—

"Tell me your hopes and dreams."

Robert laughed. Well, what sort of a question was that?

"Tell me!" Emerald slid from his arms—a sorry state of affairs, as far as Robert was concerned—and propped herself up to look at him.

He swallowed. From this perspective, he had a rather glorious view of Emerald, one he did not wish to sully with mere conversation. Why, her breasts—

"My face is here, you know."

Heat scalded Robert's cheeks. "I wasn't—"

"Yes, you were," came Emerald's gentle reproof, though she was smiling, which Robert had to assume was a good sign. "Tell me. Hopes and dreams. It's not like we haven't bared everything else."

Robert hesitated. *Hopes and dreams?* This wasn't the sort of conversation he was accustomed to, not with anyone. "Hopes and dreams?"

Emerald nodded, her eyes bright.

He swallowed. "Well, I always wanted—I wasn't sure when, or who with, but…"

He almost hoped she would interrupt him, stopping him from revealing the thoughts in his heart, but Emerald just lay there, a gentle smile on her face.

"I would like children. More than one, I am not fussy," Robert admitted. The words felt strange pouring from his mouth. *How was he saying this?*

"I should imagine not," came the wry reply. Emerald laughed as she saw his expression. "Well, it is not as though you would be doing the difficult bit!"

"No, just the enjoyable bit," agreed Robert, trying not to think of what they had shared last night. Was it possible they had not been careful enough? That they had in fact—"And a house in the country."

"Oh, yes, I would much rather live in the country than Town," said Emerald eagerly.

Robert frowned. "Have you ever lived in the country?"

She shook her head with a laugh. "But it has to be better than Town—fewer people, fewer opportunities to see people, all that walking and nature…my idea of heaven."

"And we'll have horses," said Robert, hardly aware he had shifted from the singular to the plural. "At least one each, and one for the children."

"Two for the children—I can't abide arguments."

"And a dog."

"I already have a dog." Emerald's face flushed the moment she ceased speaking.

Robert grinned. "Is that a proposal?"

Her flush deepened. "A-Absolutely not!" Emerald spluttered.

Their laughter mingled as Robert pulled her once more into his arms.

This was what he wanted. What he had always known he had wanted. What he had thought he would share with Isabelle but had been sorely disappointed. But here, with Emerald, everything was right. There was no tension in the air, no frustrations, no lies, no pretense.

Just himself, and Emerald, in bed, talking openly.

Oh, he would have to propose soon.

As Emerald settled into his arms once more, sighing happily, Robert tried not to think about the first time he proposed matrimony to a woman. Well, he could hardly have known how it would end, could he?

This time was different, and not only because he had bedded Emerald before any thought of a proposal had entered his mind.

This was true. Not true love, he was no green-gilled sap who believed in such a thing.

But truer than anything he had experienced before. Why, Emerald had already been more open, more honest with him than any woman. Any person, now he came to think about it.

In fact, he—

"Where do you think you're going?" Robert said suddenly.

To his great consternation, Emerald had done the unthinkable and had not just moved away from him but was stepping out of the bed!

Though it gave him a rather marvelous view, it could not be borne. Where did she think she was going? Were they to be parted so swiftly?

"Home, of course," Emerald said quietly. "My mother must be worried sick after I did not return home last night. Why, the gossip that may already have—"

"Let them gossip," said Robert. *Anything to keep her here, anything to prevent a parting that he knew was coming...*

Emerald raised an eyebrow, picking up her gown. "You would rather my parents worry themselves to death? You want Micah to come looking for me—or worse, Sapphy?"

Robert laughed. "Dear Lord, to have Sapphire de Petras unleashed on me!"

"So, you see why I have to go," said Emerald, pulling her gown up, ignoring her chemise and stays. "Even if...even if I do not wish to."

His heart twisted. Of course, she did not; she felt the loss as well as he did. They were attuned in such a way he had never imagined.

"They will assume you stayed overnight at Lady Romeril's," Robert said softly. He was leaning forward now, eager, hoping to show her as well as tell her just how desperately she was needed here.

Emerald's eyebrow was still raised. "You think Lady Romeril would lie for me?"

"I think we don't need to tell Lady Romeril anything," Robert said hastily.

Goodness, the inquisition he would face…

She smiled mischievously. "And if I decided to stay, what would you have in mind?"

Robert grinned. He bounded out of bed in a heartbeat, pulling the laughing Emerald into his arms and toppling the two of them onto the bed.

"Oh, many things," he whispered as he kissed her neck. "So many it may be quicker to show you…"

# CHAPTER FIFTEEN

*June 4, 1810*

E MERALD KNEW IT was scandalous to be actively seeking the company of a gentleman.

But then, it was unbelievably scandalous to have permitted herself to be bedded by him.

In truth she should have ensured, as best she could, that she did not see Robert for several days. A week. Perhaps more—anything to stop any gossip after their sudden and rather unusual…absence from Lady Romeril's ball.

The trouble was, she could not. Staying away from Robert was like deciding not to breathe. It seemed easy, in theory.

Emerald flushed as she adjusted her parasol on her shoulder as she walked along the busy pavement with Captain at her heels.

And the last thing she wanted was for everyone to notice. No, she must see Robert, she tried to convince herself as the summer heat built in London's streets, the place absolutely teeming with people. She had to see him, alone, and then it would not be so difficult when she did see him in public. At the next ball.

There was a ball in a few days, her mother had encouraged—nay, forced her—into accepting the invitation, and Emerald had to be sure that he would be there.

Excitement fluttered at her heart. He had to be there, for she had decided that for the first time in her life, if she was able to summon up the courage and convince herself, she would dance. In public. With him.

Emerald knew the way. Robert had been careful to give her his address after their assignation—hopeful, she was sure, she would wish to repeat the evening again.

And though she did, though every part of her ached to be touched and kissed by him, Emerald had managed to stay away for an entire day. Impressive, when one thought about it.

But today she had awoken in her own bed, cold and lonely, and knew. She had to see him. Had to tell him of her plan to dance with him at the ball.

A smile was on her face as Emerald turned into the quiet street of the Swindmore townhouse. Trees rustled gently in the breeze and Captain yapped at a pigeon who lazily fluttered just of her reach.

Any minute now, she would be talking to Robert—perhaps, if Emerald was fortunate, he would steal a kiss. She shivered. *Even just one kiss was enough to turn make her…*

The bellpull was an impressive brass and smelled powerfully of polish. Emerald pulled it, hearing the jangling echo from inside the house.

Her heart quickened. The moment she saw Robert—

The door opened. A tall man with a livery frockcoat and a frown opened it.

"Yes?" he said rudely.

Emerald swallowed. Fear rushed through her once more, all the excitement and joy, the anticipation of seeing Robert disappearing. Speaking to another person, being looked at by them…it was awful. How did anyone bear it?

"Are you lost, Miss?" said the butler.

Emerald attempted, as best she could, to draw herself up to her full height. "No."

She had intended to speak with far more clarity, but it appeared that was all she could manage at the moment.

Captain yapped. The butler frowned down his nose at the dog, who sat obediently, waiting for a treat.

The butler's lip curled. "If you are not lost, then you have business here?"

Emerald nodded. All she had to do was get through the butler; that would not be too difficult, would it? *Just think up anything—anything!*

"I am here to see your master," she said, her voice a little less certain than she would have liked, but she had at least spoken aloud. "Thank you."

A sardonic smile crept over the servant's face. "And do you have an appointment?"

"I…" Emerald's voice trailed off.

Well, she could not say she had an appointment if she did not have one, could she? It would be unconscionable. Besides, if she was any judge, the butler was not going to let her in.

Which was most strange. Why on earth would the servant not permit her to enter?

"No," she admitted.

The butler's smirk was irritating to behold. "As I thought. No, I am sorry to say my master is not in at present. But if you would like to leave a card…"

Emerald flushed. She had not brought a reticule, had not even thought she may have to leave a card. It was madness to think she had left the house without the basics of polite civility, but then she had hardly been in her right mind when she had flown out the door that morning, shouting to her mother she would be back in time for luncheon. Probably.

She swallowed. "Just tell him Miss de Petras called."

The butler bobbed his head rather than anything resembling civility. "Miss Peters."

"De Petras."

"Whatever," said the man dryly.

Fury bubbled in Emerald's stomach. Why did the man have to be so rude? If Sapphire was here, she would give the servant a piece of her mind, put him in his place, but as it was…

Emerald swallowed, trying to think of something witty and cutting to say, but the words simply did not come. How did they come to others? It was impossible to imagine.

The butler raised an eyebrow. "If that is all—"

"Ah, Miles, tell his lordship I will return soon, will you?"

Emerald stared. A woman perhaps a year or two older than herself wearing an elegant crisp blue muslin and a stunningly beautiful smile had appeared in the doorway, pulling a reticule onto her arm and beaming at the butler.

*Goodness.* Robert had never mentioned his housekeeper was so…so stylish. So fashionable. If any other gentleman had a servant of such beauty in his staff, Emerald was sure he would not be able to keep his hands to himself.

The butler bowed. "Of course."

He disappeared into the house, and as the woman pulled on a pair of light kid gloves, she smiled at Emerald. "And who are you here for?"

Emerald felt heat prickle her neck, hoping to goodness her cream muslin gown would not show off the red too badly. Why was it she fell to pieces when speaking to anyone? Why, she was just a housekeeper! A pretty one, that was true, but a servant. She should not have to worry about impressing the likes of her!

"I came to see his lordship," Emerald said as stiffly as she could manage.

Captain barked, evidently tired of waiting for her treat for sitting so patiently, and the woman glanced down.

"Oh, what a pretty thing!" She knelt and stroked Captain, who immediately rolled over and presented her stomach. "And so clever, too!"

*Not clever by half,* Emerald thought darkly. Really, it was most irritating having a dog better prepared for Society. At least it enabled the focus to remain away from her, as she tried to forget how irritating the butler had been.

"I do apologize, I did not listen to a whit of word you said," the woman said breezily, straightening up and smiling coldly at Emerald. "Who did you say you were here to see?"

It was most provoking. Who else could she possibly be visiting? Emerald was hardly like to be coming here to meet with a maid, was she!

"His lordship," Emerald repeated, trying to keep her voice cold. "Robert."

She knew it was a mistake the moment his name slipped from her lips. The woman went pale, despite the warmth of the day, and she stepped outside from the doorframe, forcing Emerald to step back.

"I beg your pardon," sniffed the woman haughtily, glaring as though she had mortally wounded her. "Would you like to explain just why you are here to see my husband?"

Emerald stared at the woman. Her—her husband?

A strange sort of ringing was echoing in her ears. It was too much, too nonsensical. It could not be true, the woman must be lying, jesting, teasing. Why would she say such a thing?

*"Would you like to explain just why you are here to see my husband?"*

Her husband? Robert was—he could not be her husband.

There must be a misunderstanding, Emerald was sure. Had not Robert said that he had no wish to be married? Was it not one of the reasons she had first been so drawn to him, a gentleman who understood and shared her aversion to the marital state?

"I-I beg your pardon," stammered Emerald, staring at the woman who could not be Robert's wife. "I think I misheard you for a moment there…what did you say?"

"I said, why are you here visiting my husband? Who are you? What are you to him?"

What was she to him?

Emerald hardly knew anymore. She did not know anything; all knowledge was seeping from her mind. Nothing was true, nothing could be trusted.

Robert Ainsworth, Marquess of Swindmore…married?

It did not make sense. Emerald had thought him a rake at first, assumed that as a marquess, Robert would have his pick of the ladies, of mistresses. She had thought him strange for seeking out her company, for attempting to convince her to dance with him…

And she should have trusted her instincts.

*"Why are you here visiting my husband? Who are you? What are you to him?"*

A fool, Emerald thought bitterly as Captain pulled on her lead and tried to get another pat from the woman who had ended, perhaps forever, her only chance of happiness.

Oh, Robert must have thought her a complete fool, and he would not be the only one. Why, the *ton* must have known he was married, must have thought her a flirt at best, a harlot at worst, for allowing him to force his attentions on her.

Why would he hide this? Why would he lie, keep this from her?

After all their conversations, Robert had not seen fit to mention his aversion to marriage did not preclude him from having a wife?

The Marchioness of Swindmore was looking at her carefully. "Interesting. You did not know, did you?"

Emerald shook her head slowly, not trusting her voice. The last thing she wanted to do was demonstrate just how much this revelation had shocked her to her very core.

Did not know? No, she'd had no idea Robert was playing her for a fool, that all his kisses were lies, that when he had told her he loved her, it was the second-rate love of a mistress.

A wry smile was creeping over Robert's wife's face. "Dear me. Miss de Petras, did you say? What will the gossips of Society say?"

And a terrible, painful thought rushed through Emerald as she considered this question. *Oh, there was going to be so much talk.*

The very thing she hated, the thing she attempted to avoid with every breath in her body, her nightmare, the thing she dreaded. Gossip, scandal, rumor. People would be pointing at her in the streets, the scandal sheets would be full of her.

Goodness, if it truly got out, she may even appear in the newspapers. *In the papers!*

Emerald swallowed, her throat dry, her lungs tight.

"Well, I never thought I would ever meet with one of Robert's mistresses," the marchioness said lightly, "but there you go, I suppose it was going to happen one time or another. I hope, if you do not mind me saying so, that we never meet again."

Emerald stared at the woman who already had Robert's affections, who had captured his heart. Yes, she had never wished to marry, but that had been before she had met him, been changed by him, been kissed by him…

But it was all a lie. A trick, a game, probably. Robert had probably been laughing at her when they had talked about the future, about the things they wanted…

*"And a dog."*

*"I already have a dog."*

*"Is that a proposal?"*

Emerald dropped her gaze, shame overwhelming her.

"I would ask you to leave my husband alone, but I know your kind," said the marchioness. "You're all the same, you harlots."

"I—"

"Ah, Isabelle, there you are," called someone from the street. "Ready for our walk?"

*Isabelle.*

*"Isabelle was…a woman. Just a woman. A woman I was…let us call it, involved with. But I am not anymore. Involved, I mean."*

It was too much for Emerald to bear. Pulling at Captain's lead, feet like lead and a heart thundering, she turned away from the woman who had ended all her foolish dreams—dreams she had told herself she would never have in the first place—and rushed away without paying attention to where she was going.

Her feet knew the way. Within ten minutes, eyes filled with tears, Emerald found herself stumbling into the de Petras household.

*Home.* Here, at last, she would be safe. Here she would not have to face any questions, any tormenting judgment. She could just hide away and—

"There you are," called Sapphire's voice from the parlor. The sound of terrible pianoforte music halted. "Thank goodness, I have been looking for an excuse to stop my practice for a good ten minutes, and soon I would have had to concoct something dreadful!"

Emerald said nothing. Captain's lead slid through her fingers and the dog rushed toward the sound of Sapphire's voice, leaving her owner in the hallway.

What was she going to do? How would she ever explain to her family that she was never leaving these four walls again— would her mother attempt to force her to continue with their compromise? Only three balls left, her mother would say, but Emerald knew she could never face anyone who was not her family ever again.

That part of her life was over. All she could hope now was that she could fade into dull obscurity.

"You know, I think I am going to have to make your marquess introduce me to his friends," came Sapphire's voice, the sound of the piano stool being pushed back, echoing around the house. "Micah's friends are absolute louts, you cannot trust them, and I would find it absolutely darling to be engaged at the end of my first Seas—Ems."

Emerald looked up, blinking away yet more tears. Her little sister was standing in the doorway, mouth open, a crestfallen expression on her face.

"Ems, what's the matter?" Sapphire said quietly.

Without another word, she pulled Emerald into an embrace.

The dam collapsed. Emerald sobbed into her sister's hair, clutching her as though she was the last thing keeping her on this earth. It was all over, all lies, all stupid, and she had trusted him and cared for him and loved him, and he was just like all the others. Worse, worse than the others.

A liar and a blaggard and a man she…she had truly loved.

For it was a broken heart, this dense heavy monstrosity in her chest. Emerald knew it now, all too late. That she cared for him too much, and he had repaid her by lying.

After several minutes, Emerald had cried all the tears left within her, for the present. She straightened up, brushing the last tears from her eyes, and looked blearily at her sister.

"You look awful," said Sapphire simply.

Emerald choked a laugh. "Thank you."

"What on earth is the matter?"

Emerald swallowed. To put into words the betrayal she had just endured…she would not force Sapphire to hear it. Robert did not deserve time on her lips. After today, she would never speak his name again.

"Nothing."

Sapphire frowned. "I may be the youngest, but I am not a fool, you know. Something has happened—something with Robert? If he has hurt you—"

"Sapphy."

Her sister blinked. "Yes?"

Emerald tried to steady her breathing, but even though she had just moments ago believed no more tears could fall, she was already proven to be mistaken.

"Let's not talk about him."

"Well, we don't have to go over it all now, after a bath and a hot—"

"No," Emerald interrupted, a sureness in her voice that was most unlike her. A cold, dead voice that was stagnant of all joy. "No, not after a bath. I am never going to mention that man's name again."

Sapphire stared. "Never going to—"

"And neither are you," said Emerald firmly, wiping her eyes. She would cut him from her life and cut him from her heart. "I am never going to see him again."

# CHAPTER SIXTEEN

*June 7, 1810*

*T**HE EIGHTH BALL.**

The anticipation tingling down Robert's spine could no longer be ignored. If his information was correct—and he saw no reason to disbelieve the Earl of Maltravers, who clearly knew the family well—the entire de Petras family would be here tonight. Even Micah, which apparently was to be considered some sort of miracle.

"And Miss de Petras?" Robert had asked, attempting something akin to aloofness.

"What?" The Earl of Maltravers did not appear to be listening. "Sapphire will be there, yes, I said all of them will be."

And Robert had frowned. "No, Emerald. Will Emerald be there?"

It had been all he could do not to punch the man on the nose when he replied, "Oh, I suppose so, but what difference does that make?"

Was the man jesting?

*What difference does that make?* Robert almost laughed as he started to walk about the large ballroom, eyes searching for the de Petras family. It amazed him, truly, that some people could not see the treasure Emerald de Petras was. It was as though she was invisible, quiet and demure in the corners of people's lives, but as far as he was concerned, she shone brighter than all those around her.

"Ah, your lordship!"

Robert smiled as Edward and Coral de Petras approached him. "Your Graces."

"Are you here for Emerald?" asked Coral directly, a vision in a crimson silk gown.

How was he supposed to answer such a question? Robert had no chance to think through how he would offer for her—would he ask her parents or speak to Emerald first?

But he saw no reason to lie to her sister and brother-in-law. After all, thought Robert with a rush of excitement, they would soon be his own sister and brother.

A family. Goodness, this proposal really would change his life.

"Yes," he said, forced to raise his voice as the chatter in the room grew. "Is she here?"

"If I know Emerald, they'll be late," Coral said with a laugh. "You know how she is."

Robert beamed. He did. He had believed himself knowledge-able about Isabelle when they had married yet there had been so much hidden about her, but Emerald?

No, she was an open book—one that he would willingly read for the rest of his life.

Edward had nudged his wife, who muttered, "Well! It's not as though it's a secret that Ems doesn't like balls!"

"I hope to dance with her," said Robert impulsively.

His affection for Emerald was pouring out of him, making it difficult not to speak of her. Why shouldn't he? He would be speaking about Emerald for the rest of his days.

Edward's eyes widened. "Dance?"

"With Emerald?" added his wife in astonishment. "Here?"

Robert grinned. "I have a feeling she will…"

What he had intended to say faded. Words were no longer necessary. Neither was breathing, apparently, for Robert found his chest constricted and his heart beating faster as his gaze drifted across Coral's shoulder and at the group just entering.

The de Petras family.

There was Opal and Jasper, beaming at those around them. Robert spotted Sapphire but only for a moment as she darted off to speak with an acquaintance—was that Maltravers? It was impossible to tell at this distance. The sulky gentleman behind them had to be Micah. And there was…

*Emerald.*

There was something so reassuring about Emerald. Why, she had to know that he would be here, waiting for her, ready to comfort her in this situation where she felt so uncomfortable—yet there was tension still on her face, hands clasped before her.

He stepped forward, entirely forgoing the polite niceties of taking his leave with Coral and Edward, but that did not matter. Nothing mattered. Only Emerald mattered.

"Mr. de Petras, Mrs. de Petras," murmured Robert as he reached them and bowed.

There was a sharp intake of breath from Emerald, and he grinned as he straightened up. Was she thinking what he was thinking—of their marvelous lovemaking? It was rather scandalous to be standing here so close to her family thinking about—

"Your lordship," said Opal coldly.

Robert hesitated. It was not the warm greeting he had come to expect from the matriarch of the family, and his instincts led him to look at Emerald, who was looking at her hands. It was such a natural pose for her that he did not think twice about it. But the mother, it was most unaccountable—

"Opal, let me," began her husband, who was most oddly glaring at Robert.

"No, I am the head of the household, it is my burden to bear," said Opal sternly, before turning her gaze back to Robert. "Your lordship. I will have a word with you."

"Mama," whispered Emerald without lifting her head.

He glanced between the three of them, then looked at Micah.

For no reason he could understand, the only de Petras son was glaring, too.

"Emerald?" Robert said a little uncertainly.

"Don't you speak to my daughter in that way!" hissed Opal.

Robert stared. There had been some mistake, clearly, for there was no earthly reason the de Petras family should take against him so. Why, was he not about to offer marriage to their daughter? Did they not want their next son-in-law to be a marquess?

"You!"

Robert turned as Sapphire strode toward him, abandoning her friends. He'd expected support from that quarter after she had so blatantly encouraged him to marry her sister, but he was astonished to see the youngest de Petras glaring, pointing with her stub.

"You have the audacity to—"

"Sapphire, let me deal with this," said Opal smartly. "It is not your responsibility—"

"What is going on?" Coral had joined them now, looking between her mother and Robert in quiet astonishment. "Mama, I do not understand why—"

"You are not in full possession of the facts," her mother snapped.

Robert swallowed.

*Ah.* Was it possible, then, that Emerald had admitted what they had shared? That they had made love without promises or commitment?

He looked over her mother's shoulder at the flushing Emerald and sighed. Well, he had not exacted any promises of secrecy, but truth be told, he had not expected to need to.

Still, Robert's shoulders relaxed. It was an easy enough misunderstanding, and they would certainly be welcoming him with open arms once they realized he wanted to—

"Your lordship will speak with me," Opal said, cutting through his thoughts, "or I will have satisfaction."

Robert blinked. He must have misheard. "I beg your pardon?"

"Let me, Mama," said Micah grimly. "I do little enough for the family, let me do this."

"My pistols are at home, I should have brought them with me," Jasper was muttering. "Best laid plans, and all—"

"Pistols—s-satisfaction?" Robert spluttered.

This was a dream, a nightmare! The ball was warm, and all the de Petrases were acting very strangely. Try as he might, Robert could not avoid the piercing glare of Sapphire, and while Emerald looked her normal, nervous self, Coral looked confused, now whispering urgently with her father.

"I do not understand," began Robert hesitantly. "I-I think there's been a misunder—"

"I'll give you *misunderstanding!*"

Opal stepped forward, a bitter look on her face, but she was instantly held back by her husband and eldest daughter.

"No, Mama!"

"He's not worth it, Opal, there'll be another—"

"That Italian temper, it always comes out!"

The latter speech was uttered by someone else. Robert spun around to see them.

His face fell. *Lady Romeril.* What on earth did she want?

"Now then, Opal," Lady Romeril said calmly as she stepped toward her friend. "You tell me all about it, and I will make sure my sons—"

"Am I not sufficient to defend Emerald's honor?" Micah snapped.

"But..." Robert's voice trailed away.

*This was madness.* What had got into them all? Micah was arguing with Sapphire, Lady Romeril was listening to Opal rapidly mutter something Coral was also listening to, face aghast, and from what Robert could see, Jasper was having to prevent Edward from returning home to fetch his pistols.

*Pistols? Duels—satisfaction?* This was the sort of melodrama Robert found in the newspapers, not here, right before him!

"Emerald," he said weakly.

Emerald glanced at him, eyes filled with tears. It was unaccountable. What could have happened to hurt her?

Robert did not think. Grabbing Emerald's hand and pulling her away from her family appeared to be the only rational thing he could do if he wished to understand what on earth was going on, and she put up little resistance, though a tear did trickle down her cheek.

Pulling her through the crowds, Robert tried to think desperately about where they could go to talk—actually talk—but just then, it appeared their absence was noticed.

"Emerald—Emerald's gone!"

"And so's the blighter—Swindmore, you swindler! Where are you!"

Robert did not hesitate. There was no possibility of having a conversation with the de Petras family, not while they were all under some misunderstanding. No, he would straighten it all out with Emerald, then they could return to her family together. It was the only way.

A door. Robert made for it, pulling the unresistant and silent Emerald along with him, and he slammed the door behind him.

All the noise of the ball, the music, the chatter, the shouting of the de Petras family, who were clearly confused about him though precisely how Robert did not know, faded into the background. They were left in silence, in what appeared to be a storage room. A pair of candles flickered, gifting a gentle glow to Emerald's face.

Robert's stomach twisted. Oh, she was so beautiful. So much more beautiful than he had remembered. To think, soon he would be married to—

"How dare you," Emerald said quietly.

Robert's jaw dropped. "Not you as well!"

"I have no idea what you mean," she said stiffly, wrenching her arm from his grip. "And I will thank you t-to return me to my family."

Robert stared. What in the world had happened to cause the entire de Petras family to turn against him—for Emerald to speak so coldly? Why, the last time they'd been together…

*"I want you to know that I love you. You do know that, don't you?"*

*"Yes…"*

And now this? That she could look at him with such ice in her throat, such dull eyes, as though she drew no pleasure from seeing him, no pleasure at all. What had happened?

"I don't understand," said Robert helplessly. "I—"

"You don't—you don't understand?" Emerald repeated, a flicker of fire in her tone. "And here I was thinking that I was the one who deserved explanations?"

"Ex-Explanations?"

Something terrible had happened, that was all Robert could think. Only something truly awful could have made Emerald look at him like that, as though she hated him. As though she would rather tear him apart with her bare hands than suffer his presence.

"I think you are fortunate my mother did not box your eyes," said Emerald coldly. "I had no desire to come here tonight."

"I know," said Robert, relieved to have found stable ground. "I know how you feel about balls, and—"

"You don't know me."

The four words were spoken with such anger, Robert took a step backward. Emerald was staring as though he was nothing, as though he was dirt.

"Emerald?" Robert breathed, utterly lost. "What could I have done to deserve—"

"When were you intending to tell me you were married?" Emerald shot back.

Silence hung in the air for what felt like an eternity. Robert's breath had been forced from his lungs, his mind buzzing, unable to think, as Emerald's words echoed about the room—or was it just his ears?

*"When were you intending to tell me you were married?"*

Of course. Of course, why had he not thought of it immediately? There was only one person who would wish such harm to him, only one person who held any secrets of his who could create such animosity in people who had previously held him in such high regard.

Isabelle.

"Isabelle," Robert said weakly.

Emerald turned away, but not before he noticed another tear had fallen down her cheek. "You say your wife's name to me—you astonish me."

"My wife—no, Emerald, you are mistaken!" Robert almost laughed with relief; there, finally, was the misunderstanding. To think she believed… "Isabelle is not my wife."

"Do not lie to me, your lordship. I have no desire to be treated as a fool," said Emerald bitterly, not turning to him. "At least, no more of a fool than I have been treated already."

"But I am not treating you like a—Emerald, look at me."

Robert grasped her shoulders and spun her round, but Emerald refused to meet his gaze, tears falling unchecked.

"Isabelle is not my wife," he said firmly, still gripping onto her shoulders in fear she would attempt to turn away. "She…she was once, and it was the biggest mistake of my—Isabelle and I were divorced a few months ago."

Emerald's breathing caught, and she finally looked at him. "So, you lied about being divorced."

"I did not—omitting to tell you—"

"It is a lie if you kiss me and tell me you love me, and bed me, and do not tell me that you have been divorced just months before!" Emerald said, pain in her voice.

Robert swallowed. Well, when she put it like that…but did she not see, he had no interest in Isabelle, had made that quite clear by the fact that he had divorced her!

He took a deep breath. "I had no wish to dwell on such a painful part of my—"

"I cannot believe you would not volunteer that information when I asked you to…" Emerald's voice trailed away, her cheeks flushing as she recalled her request.

That request had brought them both so much happiness.

*"I want you to make love to me."*

"It's not as though I thought you expected me to bring up every dark and sorry part of my past!" Robert said, almost laughing at the thought. "You think everything should be shared, so quickly?"

"I shared much about myself," Emerald shot back, pulling herself free of his hands.

"Well, you did not have nearly so much to confess," Robert said, temper rising.

What, was he supposed to be apologizing now for being married? He felt sorry enough in the first place for being saddled with Isabelle so long—and Emerald thought *she* was the one who deserved the apology?

"I thought you had been honest!"

"And I honestly did not think it was any of your business!" Robert knew he should stop, should take a breath, and attempt to collect his thoughts before he spoke, but pain was radiating through his heart and could not be stopped.

Had he not suffered enough? Was he about to lose the only woman he had ever truly loved, merely because he had been a fool as a youth and married someone entirely wrong for him?

"You were my business!" Tears sparkled in Emerald's eyes. "I opened myself to you, made myself vulnerable—far more vulnerable than I have ever been in my—"

"Everyone has a past!"

"I don't!" Emerald stated firmly.

Robert threw up his hands, turning away, unable to look at the woman who he loved and yet seemingly did not wish to give him the time of day. "Well, of course, you don't."

He should halt his tongue and attempt to discuss this another time, Robert knew, but heat was blossoming through his veins, and he could not believe Emerald could so quickly believe the worst of him.

Believe he was still married? That he was lying to her, hiding a wife?

"And what," came Emerald's pained voice, "is that supposed to mean?"

Knowing he would be better served by leaving this moment, Robert barreled on, hardly caring now what he said.

What difference would it make? Emerald had decided against him; her family had decided against him. Why did they think he had hidden his past in the first place?

He'd had enough of being judged for getting it wrong the first time—especially as he had been so sure he had got it right the second time!

Emerald de Petras. They could have made each other so happy.

"I mean," Robert said harshly, "that it is your family that has a past, not you. Your family is full of secrets and scandal—I've heard about the letters! I've heard about the sudden wealth your mother inherited, though she had a brother, and most mysterious it certainly is!"

Emerald gasped, her mouth falling open, but Robert wasn't finished. The floodgates had opened now, and there was nothing he could do to prevent the tirade of pain from lashing out.

"And you don't have a past, Emerald, because you have never done anything in your life worth gossiping about! And that may keep you safe," Robert said, stepping toward her, "and that may keep you out of the scandalous newspapers, but it also means you know nothing of the world, nothing of what you want, and nothing of your own heart!"

He was so close to her now, he could kiss her. Robert was panting, heart pounding, and as Emerald looked up at him, lips parted, he was visited by a strong desire to kiss her.

His head started to lower just as Emerald stepped aside and rushed toward the door.

"Well, as I have done nothing of note, I am sure you will understand that I must return to the ball and start some scandals of my own," came her pained words.

The door slammed. Robert was left alone. Alone, save his own bitter regret.

# CHAPTER SEVENTEEN

*June 12, 1810*

"ABSOLUTELY OUTRAGEOUS! THE more I think about it, the more angry I—"

"Then don't think about it," Emerald murmured.

It did not matter. She was not paid attention to as she had not been from the moment they had all returned from the ball which had ended in such disaster.

*"Well, as I have done nothing of note, I am sure you will understand that I must return to the ball and start some scandals of my own."*

Emerald closed her eyes, as though that could force from her mind the cruel words thrown at her by the man she had thought she loved. The man she had thought loved her.

*"Now I know that…that I have never been in love. Not until I met you."*

But what did that matter? Words, words, they were easy to spill from the lips and hurl in an argument. How could she trust them? How could she trust anything Robert—that man—had said?

"To think, I really thought he was a man to be trusted—nay, a man who could be relied upon to—"

"Yes, Coral," mumbled Emerald.

It was exhausting, sitting as her sister droned on and on about how they had all been tricked, lied to by that scheming marquess. As though she wanted to hear any more about it! As though she did not wish she could abandon all thoughts of Robert—*that man*—to the past.

Emerald swallowed. *If only that were possible.* Not only was her heart in direct rebellion, constantly reminding her of the pleasant conversations they had shared, the moments of intimacy which had been like walking in someone else's life.

A life that was ripped from her the moment it was all getting too…too wonderful.

Coral rose from the armchair in the large saloon of the Glaenarm townhouse and started to pace up and down, throwing her hands about as she spoke.

"We should never have trusted him—I mean, what did we know of him, really? Very little, and as I told Mama just last week, we needed to be careful about such gentlemen. I mean, yes, we knew little of Edward before we married, and I was a little confused about the exact nature of his wealth…"

It was usually just easier to let Coral get it out of her system—at least, that had always been Emerald's approach when they had been children. It was far more trying now, as grown women, when one was forced to endure endless Coral monologues.

"—just outrageous! I tell you, we should have had him investigated, we certainly will look into any suitors for Sapphire most closely. Why, if a marquess can lie to you, lie to your face like that—"

It had been her mother's idea to visit Coral today. Something to get her out of the house, Opal had said. *Something to stop you from stewing all alone at home.*

Emerald had felt the unspoken criticism like a bullet into her shoulder. *All alone.*

Yes, she was all alone, and now she had been so roundly deceived by the one man she had thought she could trust. She was likely to remain alone for some time. The maiden aunt, the spinster aunt, the one no one wished to marry…

"And Edward had spoken to him already, warning him not to—"

"Not to what?" Emerald sat up straighter. "Edward spoke to him?"

Coral halted in her seemingly endless strides back and forward, a hint of guilt in her eyes. "Did I say that?"

"You most certainly did," said Emerald. "Coral. Do not try to hide the truth from me—you think I have not had enough of that, these last few days?"

She regretted her words the moment she spoke them. It was unfair to throw that at her sister. It was not Coral's fault Robert had been such a—a liar!

"I did not mean to say…it was only…" Coral sighed and sat theatrically on the armchair. "Only that your marquess—"

"He is not my marquess," Emerald said, heat searing her cheeks.

He could have been.

She may have supposed he would consider…she had said she had no desire to marry, but perhaps he had not heeded her.

Perhaps he did not care. He had not thought it important to tell her anything important, after all.

"*The* marquess, then," said Coral bad-temperedly.

Emerald did not rise to the bait. It was on her account, after all, that the family was so fractious at the moment. Robert's fault. Somewhere between them, the fault lay, though if you asked her, it was primarily on his side.

She had not lied. By omission, anyway.

She had not been married before.

She did not have a secret wife—ex-wife—still traipsing in and out of her home as though she owned the place…

"Edward spoke to him briefly at the club a few weeks ago," said Coral, waving a hand as though her husband chattered to lying, scheming cheats all the time. "Merely to warn him to leave you alone, Emerald. That was all."

Hot embarrassment flooded Emerald's veins. "Did Edward think I needed protection?"

"From any gentleman, really," said Coral, clearly not comprehending the hurt this caused in her sister's heart. "You are delicate, Emerald, you do not understand—"

"I understand a great deal more than you might think," Emerald cut across.

Really, was she to endure such mockery! Did no one in her family think her able to navigate the world—did they really think her so foolish, so easily led...

Emerald's jaw tightened, and all possibility of speech disappeared.

Perhaps she was a fool. She had been foolish enough to allow that cad to speak horrendous things about her family, right to her face! She should have stopped him in his tracks, forced him to apologize for saying such outrageous things...but she had been unable to. The onslaught of words, so painful...

*"I've heard about the sudden wealth your mother inherited, though she had a brother, and most mysterious it certainly is!"*

"—and all Edward thought he was doing was protecting you, for who knows what sort of men are out there, and in hindsight, it is perfectly clear your marquess—"

"Not my marquess," Emerald said automatically. "What do you know about Mama?"

Coral blinked, her protective tirade about her husband halted. "I beg your pardon?"

"About her past, I mean," amended Emerald, nerves twisting at her heart, but she had to know. She had to ask. And Coral was their mother's heir. If there was anything to know... "About how she became so wealthy. About a brother—do you know anything about threatening letters?"

Her sister's eyes were wide. "Threatening—"

"If you have questions, my dear, I ask that you bring them to me," came the cool, collected voice of Opal de Petras.

Emerald spun around in her seat. There in the doorway to

the hall, the majestic staircase and chandelier still visible past her shoulder, was her mother. There was a steely glint in her eyes that Emerald rarely saw, and it did not bode well.

She swallowed. She really should have asked her mother directly, should she not? Being overheard asking her sister about it…well, it was tantamount to gossip! What if Opal thought she was stirring trouble or—

"Mama, I am sure Emerald did not mean anything by the question," said Coral hastily, confirming Emerald's suspicions that there was something to uncover.

Secrets in the family? Surely not. The de Petras family was open—arguably too open. All in all, there was always plenty of gossip, plenty of laughter, plenty of noise in her family…but secrets?

"I just wondered…" Emerald swallowed. There was nothing wrong in her asking, was there? It was just a question. "I have heard things, Mama."

Opal sniffed as she stepped into the saloon. "Things from that marquess of yours, I'll be bound."

"He is not my marquess," Emerald said.

Her mother raised an eyebrow as she sat opposite her daughter. "Indeed."

"I overheard people talking at a ball, weeks ago," said Emerald.

The trouble was, she had not put the two together.

*"I heard the mother gained her fortune through stealth or some criminal activity—"*

*"Your family is full of secrets, and scandal—I've heard about the letters! I've heard about the sudden wealth your mother inherited, though she had a brother, and most mysterious it certainly is!"*

Was it possible…

Emerald met her mother's gaze and saw sternness there, determination… fear.

"Coral, would you be a dear and leave us?" asked Opal pleasantly.

The eldest de Petras's mouth fell open. "This is my house!"

"I know," said their mother, not taking her eyes from Emerald who was starting to find the focus rather difficult to bear. "And I am asking you, politely, if you would leave us."

Emerald's gaze fell to her hands in her lap, but even without looking up, she could tell there was a completely silent conversation occurring between her mother and sister.

Less than a minute later, skirts swished to her left, the door closed, and Emerald was left alone with her mother.

It was not a comforting situation. After the devastation of Robert's betrayal, the last thing Emerald needed was more revelations to quake the very foundation of who she was.

*Her mother, a criminal? A brother? Threatening letters?*

"Well then, Emerald?" said Opal lightly. "I believe you had some questions for me."

Emerald swallowed, but there was nothing for it now but to ask. How could she sleep at night, unsure of what the truth was, now that allegations had been made?

She may be the contrary debutante, but that would be nothing if her mother was what the whispers said…

"Do you have a brother?" she asked quietly.

Her mother hesitated only for a moment. "Yes."

Emerald waited. "And?"

"And what?"

"Mama, you know what!" Emerald said, frustration pouring into her voice. "Do you not think I am done with being lied to? Do you not think I deserve the truth?"

A flicker of pain passed across Opal's face. "The truth. And what if it is none of your concern, Emerald? What if it is nothing to do with you—what if, moreover, it would do nothing but harm you to know things you cannot do a thing about? Things you would have been much happier not knowing?"

Emerald opened her mouth, tried desperately to think of a reply, then closed it again.

Her mother was breathing a little heavily, as though she had run a great distance. "That is the trouble with the truth, Emerald. Truth? Whose truth? Truth about what—moments that matter to some but are inconsequential for others?"

"I just want to know," said Emerald weakly. Why was it so difficult for anyone to give her a straight answer? "There is talk of threatening letters, a-and criminal wealth, and—"

"And my brother."

She stared. Opal de Petras had never spoken before about a brother, though now she came to think of it, Emerald could not recall her mother ever talking about any members of her family.

It was strange, it was outrageous, and it was…perhaps, none of her business.

"My brother and I had a falling out some years ago," said her mother quietly. "Before you were born. Before I was married. A falling out that I regret, in a way, but it has no reflection on us as a family, and you should not worry about it."

"Not worry about—"

"As I said," Opal murmured. "None of your concern."

Something fired within Emerald at those words. None of her concern? Why did everyone else get to decide what was her concern, and what was not?

"It is my concern," she said fiercely. "It's my family—you are my mother, Mama, and if Society knows some gossip about us, about you that I am going to be forced to endure—"

"You are my responsibility," interrupted her mother, eyes bright.

"But that does not mean we should never care about you."

Emerald was not entirely sure where the words had come from, but they were true. Opal de Petras was always caring for them, always offering counsel, always supporting them. But who was looking after her?

Opal cleared her throat loudly, and Emerald looked up. Was it her imagination, or were those tears in her mother's eyes? Surely not!

"Years ago," said Opal quietly, "years and years ago, when

you were very small—before Sapphire was even born…there were these letters."

Emerald stayed silent. She could see the pain in her mother's face, hear her agony.

"These letters threatened us, all of us, unless your father abandoned us, and I am almost certain they were written by…by my brother. My estranged brother," said Opal with no flicker of emotion in her voice now. The mask had returned.

Emerald leaned forward. "Your brother."

It was unthinkable. True, Micah was not particularly warm toward his family—though he had threatened to shoot Robert, which Emerald had to say counted for something—but to think about harming one's own?

It was unconscionable. And her mother had such a brother?

"And the money?" Emerald asked, unable to help herself.

The moment was broken. Opal cleared her throat, looked away, and when she returned her gaze to her daughter, it was warm and pleasant and lighthearted once more. As though nothing had ever happened.

"Oh, money, everyone gets themselves in knots over money," Opal said easily.

Emerald frowned. "Mama."

"Today is not the time," said her mother swiftly.

"But your brother, these letters—are you not going to find him, understand why—"

"No," Opal said firmly.

Any other day, Emerald would have accepted that as an answer. Why argue, why draw attention to yourself, why make demands of people that would only increase their focus on you?

But after discovering the truth about Robert—a truth he had attempted to keep hidden—Emerald was no longer going to accept pitter-patter, lies, half-truths. Not anymore. Not from her mother.

"Why not?" Emerald pressed.

"Because," her mother said dryly, "I have bigger problems.

Talk to me about this marquess of yours."

"He is not—"

"Yes, I know, he is not your marquess," said Opal. "And why is that?"

Emerald stared. Her mother had been told about Robert's wife the moment Sapphire had attempted to calm her that terrible day she had met Isabelle coming out of his home. Did she not understand? Had she not wished to protect her at that foolish ball—the ball she had told them she was not attending, though much difference that made.

"You cannot be serious," said Emerald, wide-eyed. "He was married!"

"Yes," said her mother calmly. "He was."

Even the confirmation of it from her mother caused pain to rush through Emerald's heart. He had been married, had lied. Robert had known everything about her, had welcomed her into his bed…and still, he could not tell her the full story of his past?

"I don't think you have heard the full story."

Emerald laughed. "That is precisely the problem."

"Stop and think, Emerald."

She looked at her mother in astonishment. "I never thought you would be defending him! After what he—"

"You told me he was married, and that was not quite the full story, was it," Opal pointed out, most irritatingly, in Emerald's opinion. "A man who was once married can marry again."

"Not to me," said Emerald bitterly.

"And why precisely is that?"

How could her mother be saying such things? How could anyone expect her to love—to even try to care for a gentleman who refused to tell her the truth?

"Emerald," said her mother gently. "Every relationship, every marriage is…Jasper is a wonderful man, but things have not always been perfect. Many people are unhappy with their spouses. Sometimes one of them will do terrible things, unforgivable things, and then the best thing to do is divorce. Not everyone can be as fortunate as myself and your sister."

Emerald swallowed. "It is not that I have no sympathy for—it is not Robert, I mean the marquess being divorced that is...he did not tell me!"

That was it, the crux of the matter, the reason why her heart was so bruised, so pained. The lack of honesty, after she had been so vulnerable, pushed past her fears...

"It is the lying," Emerald said quietly, unable to look at her mother. "He lied to me, Mama, and I tried to—I had tried so hard to be open, to...I mean, how can I believe him now?"

*"Now I know that...that I have never been in love. Not until I met you."*

She pushed aside the memory. She could not believe him. She never could.

"And I am sure it came as a shock to discover he had not been as open as you would wish," her mother said delicately. "But...Emerald, would you want someone to know all your fears, your concerns, the mistakes you've made which you wish you could undo...would you want them all in the open, from the moment of meeting someone?"

A twist of shame tore at Emerald's heart. "No, but—"

"So, when is the perfect time?" persisted Opal. "After a first dance?"

"No, that would be—"

"After a first kiss, then?"

Emerald flushed, but her mother did not look away, nor look ashamed.

"Perhaps when he proposed matrimony, then?" she asked lightly. "Would you consider that the proper time?"

All these questions whirled around Emerald's mind, and they were painful, causing shoots of uncertainty to rush up her spine.

What would the right time have been? When he'd first kissed her? When they'd left Almack's together—when Isabelle's name had first been mentioned between them?

*"Isabelle was...a woman. Just a woman. A woman I was...let us*

*call it, involved with. But I am not anymore. Involved, I mean."*

"As far as I am aware," said Opal delicately, "your marquess—the marquess, my apologies—had not proposed matrimony. Not yet, at any rate. Do you not think it likely he would have taken that opportunity to reveal the pain in his past?"

Emerald swallowed. She had not thought of that, but now her mother had mentioned it, that did make rather more sense.

*"And you don't have a past, Emerald, because you have never done anything in your life worth gossiping about!"*

Her heart hardened. "Mama, he said such things—"

"And is it possible he was hurt? That you in turn had said some words you now regret? Could it be," said her mother softly, "that he was merely trying to protect his heart?"

Emerald stared. *Oh, it was all so complicated, so painful…*

"He…" she swallowed, trying to bring her thoughts together. "He always seemed so strong. So happy."

"Perhaps that is the problem," Opal said with a sad smile. "Those who feel the need always to be strong are not very good at being weak."

# CHAPTER EIGHTEEN

*June 20, 1810*

T*HE NINTH BALL.*

If this did not go to plan, Robert knew he would never attend a ball ever again.

Almack's was heaving, as usual. Ladies chattering about the end of the Season, how sorry they were for those unmarried, unbetrothed, and left behind—a few of them, not for the first time…

Chatter about horse races, and hunts, and just how unbearable Town was at this time of year, though that of course did not stop them from staying. Chatter about weddings with the right people not invited, and hushed up scandals simply not hushed up enough, and so-and-so's gambling habit that his mother really was going to have to put a stop to…

Robert ignored it all. He could have heard his own name and unless it was paired with a certain someone, he could not care.

Not with his own words ringing in his ears, a devastating indictment on his character that he had brought upon himself, after all.

*"And you don't have a past, Emerald, because you have never done anything in your life worth gossiping about!"*

Robert's jaw tightened as he meandered around the ballroom, looking for one face—or perhaps more accurately, one family.

Not that he deserved to see them. Dear God, after the way he had behaved the last time he had been with Emerald, Robert wasn't sure whether he deserved life.

The things he had said to her…

Though he would like to justify himself with the excuse that he had been angry, and Emerald had been impossible, and it had all been Isabelle's fault in the first place…

It was his own folly, his own harshness that had injured the woman he loved. If there was any justice in the world, he would never see her again to rectify it.

His heart contracted painfully.

He had heard murmurs, at the Dulverton Club, that they would be here. The de Petrases. The last Almack's of the Season, he could not imagine Opal would forbid Sapphire's attendance. And someone would have to come with her, wouldn't they?

Emerald.

"Yes, Emerald de Petras…"

Robert's head spun around. It was Lady Romeril, and she was talking with a pair of rather irritatingly handsome gentlemen. Her sons? More godchildren of the woman who could break reputations by the merest hint of scandal?

"Miss de Petras is quite beautiful, though shy," Lady Romeril continued loudly, and before Robert could move, his gaze had met hers. Her eyes narrowed, and she did not release his gaze. "Ill-treated she has been, but I do not believe the blaggard has the gall to approach her again. I could certainly tell him what for if I had the inclination. But I never have the time to waste on wastrels, nor the desire to tell the undesirable where to go."

Robert swallowed, heart skipping a beat at the painful words, then managed to wrench away his gaze and turn from the woman who was so elegantly destroying his character.

Even if she did not name him, no one would rest until they had the full story, and he did not doubt she would eagerly give it.

His hands had clenched into fists, and it was all he could do to step away without saying something foolish.

Lady Romeril did not have the full story. No one did, not even himself. Why, there had been nights when he had lain awake, drenched in sweat, trying desperately to understand how the whole thing had collapsed so completely before his—

"Robert Ainsworth. My, my."

Robert's stomach lurched, but it was not the pleasant excitement that had filled it since he had first met Emerald de Petras.

Oh no, this was quite a different emotion, one he'd thought he would not be forced to suffer for the rest of his life. A sense of panic, of pain, of knowing one's calm exterior had to be maintained no matter the provocation.

Slowly, very slowly, Robert turned on the balls of his feet to see a woman smiling and fluttering a fan.

"Isabelle."

She smiled. "I see you are already in the throes of love. How very touching. The plain, dull girl I met?"

Robert took an unconscious step forward. "Emerald is neither plain nor dull."

"I have not the words for such an inconsequential individual," said Isabelle flatly, folding away her fan and closing the gap between them.

The crush at Almack's was starting to build, and so it was only natural, to an onlooker, that they would grow closer to converse—but Robert hated it with every fiber of his being. He had never wanted to be this close to Isabelle again. That part of his life was over, done for—*at her request!*—and he had expected to be free of her cloying attention for the rest of his days.

His heart twisted. But then, he'd had many hopes for what his life could look like, and all hopes had been dashed to pieces the moment Emerald had walked out that door.

*"That may keep you out of the scandalous newspapers, but it also means you know nothing of the world, nothing of what you want, and nothing of your own heart!"*

"Really, Robert, you do fall in love with the strangest of people," sneered Isabelle. "I think you were better off fawning over me than making a fool of yourself with that—"

"Speak another word and I am sorry to say it will be your last," said Robert curtly. He'd had enough of this, enough of her. It was time to end this, once and for all. "We are divorced, Isabelle."

She gasped, her eyes widening. "Do not say such—"

"It is the truth, and I should have said it louder and to as many people as possible a long time ago," Robert interrupted, fire soaring through his bones. "I had the opportunity to tell a woman that I—that she was everything to me. And you ruined it, Isabelle, as I should have known you would. But I will not permit you to slander the name of a good woman. You may not recognize one, but I will permit no one to say otherwise."

Perhaps Isabelle spoke; perhaps she attempted to argue with him. Robert could not tell. The moment the last word was out of his mouth, he had turned away.

Lady Romeril was watching. Was she closer? Had she heard what he had said?

In a way, it did not matter. Robert was not fool enough to believe Lady Romeril would act as his champion for his cause with the de Petras family. No, he had burnt many a bridge there, and his only hope, if they attended Almack's tonight, was to give his apology and then leave Town forever.

*"That may keep you out of the scandalous newspapers, but it also means you know nothing of the world, nothing of what you want, and nothing of your own heart!"*

Robert dropped his gaze, just for a moment, as shame and regret flooded through him. No man who had said such things to a lady, let alone Emerald, deserved her hand.

No, he would return to the country obscurity from which he came and be grateful that he had lost only his heart.

"There she is!"

"You really think the de Petras fortune is from ill-gotten

gains?"

"No woman without a past is that rich…"

Despite himself, despite his better nature, knowing it would only bring him heartache to see the family which he could have belonged to, Robert turned around.

He staggered, heart racing, palms hot as he saw not one, but two de Petrases step into Almack's.

Sapphire de Petras had unusually pink cheeks and had tucked her stub under her arm. Robert gritted his teeth. *Someone must have said something to her—incorrigible rakes!*

And beside her…

Beside her, the epitome of what a woman should be. Not that shyness was required, or beauty, or any particular characteristic. Robert could not describe the peak of womanhood, only to say he had seen the perfect mixture of bravery and nervousness, boldness and shyness, beauty and a complete lack of regard for Society's cares all wrapped up in one woman.

And she was standing there, glancing around Almack's, clearly terrified yet here.

Robert's heart raced. Emerald. She had come, despite her fears, despite her probable anxiety of seeing him…because she had made a promise. She had an agreement with her mother, and she was going to keep it.

If Robert had not already been in love with her before, he was now. How was any other woman supposed to compete with her?

"—scandalous, I call it," muttered someone behind him.

"Caught in a room with a gentleman, and still unmarried!"

"I heard it was a duke—"

"I heard a marquess—"

"So why is Emerald de Petras here? How can she hold her head up high?"

Robert did not hesitate. The gossip was only going to increase, despite Lady Romeril's best efforts, and he had nothing to lose now. He had already lost the one thing he truly wanted—Emerald's affections—so he would make good his apology and leave.

In an extraordinarily short amount of time, Robert had neared the two sisters. His stomach lurched as Sapphire caught his gaze, her mouth falling open.

Would she pull her sister away, protect Emerald from the indignity of his company?

Robert watched as Sapphire's hand took Emerald's, but before she could say anything, he was standing before them.

"Miss de Petras," was what he intended to say.

That was all. A mere statement of fact, Emerald could not argue with that.

But she did not need to. Despite Robert's best efforts, all that seemed able to emerge from his mouth was gargling noise.

Crimson stained Emerald's cheeks as she dropped her gaze. "My lord."

Robert closed his mouth and tried to concentrate, but how could anyone do such a thing with such elegant beauty before him?

He had lost the best thing that had ever been presented to him—lost her, and all hope of happiness. But could he try to explain, try to show her perhaps just how much he—

His eyes caught hers. He saw within them the fear of precisely what was going through his mind. *A grand gesture. Heaven help us, a dance. A declaration.*

The sorts of things Emerald would absolutely loathe.

A wry smile crept across Robert's lips. He knew her, better than perhaps she knew herself, but even he had almost slid into the habit of doing what other ladies would have liked. After all, what woman did not crave a dramatic apology before the rank and file at Almack's? Who did not wish to hear a speech, given in public, of how beautiful, how elegant they were?

Emerald. Emerald did not.

"Come with me," Robert said, offering his hand.

Emerald stared at his hand. Hesitancy was not the word; she appeared absolutely convinced she would not take it.

In a swift movement, Sapphire lifted Emerald's hand, which was enclosed in hers, deposited it unceremoniously on Robert's, and grinned.

"Go and talk," she said quietly. "Outside is best. Go on."

Robert needed no further encouragement, but unlike all their past private encounters, this time he would not pull Emerald from her family so he could benefit from her company.

No. This time he waited. Waited for her to make a decision.

Emerald swallowed, as though she was desperately attempting to think in the noise and hubbub of Almack's—and then she was walking, her hand still in his, back the way she came, back through the entrance way, out onto the street.

Emerald dropped his hand. "Well?"

Robert blinked. "I beg your pardon?"

She glared. "You asked me to come with you. Well?"

*Ah.* If only he had some sort of plan beyond "be in Emerald's presence for as long as he could possibly manage." That was not really a plan, was it?

"I...uh..."

"I thought, back there, for a moment that you would...that you might..." Emerald swallowed and stepped away from him.

Robert's heart sank. She had managed what, ten seconds in his company? Was he really so repellent—or had his words, spoken in anger at their last meeting, truly ended all possibility of—

"Come on," Emerald shot back over her shoulder.

He blinked. *She—she wanted him to accompany her?*

Striding forward to catch up, it quickly became evident that Emerald was merely seeking somewhere a little more private. Almack's was still welcoming late comers, after all, and the street just to the left was far quieter. The evening air was just as warm, the hazy twilight still casting a glow around Emerald's chestnut hair.

She halted, turning to face him. "Well?"

Robert swallowed. *If only I'd had a speech prepared!* "What were you going to say?"

"Oh." Emerald flushed again, and Robert tried desperately not to notice how pretty she looked, nor how her décolletage blushed along with her cheeks. "I was just going to—I thought, in Almack's, that you were going to—"

"Make a scene?" suggested Robert.

He could see the truth in her eyes immediately. She had feared it.

"A grand gesture, or-or something like that," Emerald said quietly, her gaze dropping to her clasped hands. "I do not think I would survive—"

"I know." No matter how much he longed to step forward, to take those hands once again in his, Robert managed to resist. "I know you, Emerald. I would never do that to you."

She glanced up, pain and longing mingled in her eyes, and Robert could see she still cared about him. That was what she felt, wasn't it? Or was it possible he was seeing merely what he wished to see?

Robert sighed heavily. Well, he had promised himself that he would make an apology, then leave the de Petras family to their own devices for the rest of their lives. All that was left was his apology. But how could he cover so much wrong with just one apology?

He drew a deep breath. Emerald met his gaze.

"I was wrong," Robert said simply.

She waited for a moment, then said, "Wrong."

"Wrong about so many things—wrong about Isabelle to start with—"

He should not have mentioned her name. Robert saw how the three syllables inflicted pain upon the woman he loved, Emerald flinching as the name was spoken.

"Wrong not to tell you about her," Robert added hastily. "Wrong to say such things...things I should never have said, never have permitted to—"

"I said some terrible things, too," Emerald said quietly.

He laughed dryly. "Nothing I did not deserve, I am sure, but I—I spoke ill of you and your family, Emerald, and for that, I will never forgive myself."

Contrition poured into his tone, but Robert was not sure whether it was enough. How did one take back words like that? How did you wipe away the pain caused by one's own lips?

"I've been so wrong, but worst of all…I was wrong to keep my divorce a secret from the world now that I come to reflect on it. I was so…embarrassed."

Emerald blinked. "Embarrassed? You?"

"I wanted my marriage to be a success, as so many others are," Robert admitted. Where had these secrets come from? How was it possible that just by standing there, by looking at him, Emerald could reach into his heart and make clear to him emotions he had never understood before? "To fail at something that seemed as easy to others as breathing…"

"I still do not understand why you could not tell me," Emerald said in a low voice.

Her eyes had not left him, and Robert swallowed as he tried to think of an answer that would make the most sense, that would keep him in a positive light in her eyes.

But instead, he decided on the truth. "I…damnit, Emerald, you are so…so—"

"So what?" Emerald took a hesitant step away, uncertainty once more flooding her face.

"So perfect," Robert breathed.

Her eyebrows rose at that. "You cannot possibly—you cannot mean—"

"Oh, I most certainly do," he said heavily. Why couldn't she see it? "Emerald, in all our conversations, all our meetings…when I made love to you—" her gaze darted about them, but they were perfectly alone "—I could not have known how devoted I would become to you. Emerald, I told you before that I loved you, but now I can see that the more I fell in love with you, the more…well, desperate I became to be perfect in your eyes. But perfection…it's a standard I cannot live up to."

Emerald stared, then took a step toward him. Only a foot kept them apart. "I…I will admit that I had a rather idealized view of you when we first met. Each time I encountered you, you seemed more than perfect. Too good to be true, as my mother would say."

Robert laughed. "Well, she would be right on that score."

"But your life wasn't perfect, was it?" Emerald whispered.

*Perfect?* No, Robert could not think of a more imperfect word to describe it. But it was hard to reveal the inner workings of his soul, hard to admit he was so wrong, so hurt before…

But if he could not open himself, be as vulnerable as she had with him, what hope did he have?

"Emerald, I—I told you before I had never been in love, not before you, and that is true. But I…" Robert swallowed. "I have had my heart broken. I have been betrayed by someone I trusted most dearly. My wife—my ex-wife, I should say—knew precisely how to hurt me. And she…her infidelity felt like an indictment on me. I was not a sufficient husband, she had to go…well. Elsewhere. And I felt like I was nothing, no man, not worthy of any woman's time, and each moment with you was a blessing, a privilege, and I thought if I told you, it would somehow despoil, perhaps ruin…"

A softness, a warmth in his hands. Robert blinked. Emerald had taken his hands.

"Why did you not tell me that?" Emerald asked quietly, her green eyes flashing with an emotion he did not recognize. "Any of it? All of it?"

She was the anchor, and he the ship, battered and beleaguered, desperate to reach home.

"It's hard to admit someone you cared for could leave you," he admitted softly. "I was afraid…I thought you would leave me, too. And you did."

"Because you did not tell me," Emerald reminded him gently. "You created your own downfall."

Robert choked in a laugh and pulled Emerald closer into his arms, needing to feel her, needing to know she was near. The warmth of her against him revived him, awoke something in him that he thought had died a long time ago.

"But I love you, Emerald," he murmured, "and I knew if I lost you—"

"Then you had better marry me," Emerald breathed, a shy smile on her lips. "And that way, you'll never lose me again."

The kiss was warm and welcoming, just what Robert needed. Almost sobbing with relief that he had her, despite all his foolishness, despite the secrecy, despite his own foolishness, Robert captured Emerald's lips and worshipped them, ravishing her mouth for pleasure and giving back just as much in return.

Finally, all too soon, the kiss ended.

Emerald blinked. "And they called me contrary."

Robert laughed, tightening his grip around her. "Debutante no longer. Goodness, I never would have thought this evening would return to you to me!"

"No," she agreed with mischief in her eyes. "Though we now have to overcome a far greater challenge."

His stomach lurched. "We do?"

Emerald nodded, laughing now as she kissed the corner of his lips. "We need to explain it all to my family."

# CHAPTER NINETEEN

*June 22, 1810*

*T*HE TENTH BALL.

"You really must calm down!" laughed Robert as Emerald leaned toward the window of the carriage once more. "You won't make the carriage go any faster!"

"But it's the last one!" Emerald said impulsively, smiling a little shyly, still, at the gentleman she was going to marry in just a few weeks. "You do not understand—you cannot possibly understand what it feels like to know that after today, I never have to go to a ball again!"

It was difficult not to laugh with exultation.

Not merely because she would never have to go to a ball again, though Emerald had to admit that the thought was spectacular. Never have to pull on an uncomfortable gown, drown oneself in heavy or discomforting jewels—jewels you were terrified all night you would lose—be forced to speak with unpleasant people, struggle to hear people over the noise of the music or, worst of all, actually be asked to dance...

No, it was because of the gentleman next to her.

"Must our daughters really take your name? And my wife shall not take my name?" he'd asked in a voice he had clearly thought was quiet.

Emerald had winced at the time. Just an hour before, when they had been finishing the final preparations before they left for the tenth ball in her agreement, Robert had asked her that question, and she had been willing to answer.

The trouble was, he had asked it in the drawing room of her home. And that meant they were surrounded by—

"Not give your daughters the de Petras name?" Emerald's mother had said, mouth open. "I never heard of such a thing!"

"The best people do it," Edward had grinned.

Sapphire had laughed.

"Sapphire!"

The chorus of outrage had come from both her sisters and her mother, but that did not seem to stop the incorrigible youngest de Petras.

After all her fears, frustrations, and determination never to be married, Emerald had found a man who was worthy of all that pain.

Something she had not believed possible.

"There'll be talk, you know."

*There would be talk.*

Emerald de Petras, the middle child of the outrageous de Petras family—engaged to be married to a marquess? That quiet thing, everyone would say. That shy, retiring, uninteresting girl, capture the attention of a titled nobleman?

Her heart was pattering again most painfully, but there did not appear to be anything she could do about it.

The carriage bumped over a stone in the road, and Emerald's stomach lurched, far more than one would expect.

There would be talk, and it would be all about her.

Perhaps people would point. Perhaps they would—

"We're almost there," said Robert quietly.

Emerald glanced out of the window. He was right. The Duke of Larnwick's London townhouse was only a few minutes away.

Steeling her nerves, she tightened her grip on Robert's hands. He seemed to understand, squeezing them back.

Some of the tension in her shoulders melted away. He did understand. And he would always be by her side, always protecting her, always there to support her during these awful moments when the world was watching.

The carriage slowed as it turned a corner, and Emerald took a deep breath. It was a relief, really, that Robert had insisted the two of them travel in their own carriage.

Not that she had anything against her family. But being wedged into a carriage with her mother, her father, her sisters, and a brother-in-law—and Micah, though he had not deigned to arrive in time—was not something Emerald would have chosen before the last ball she would ever attend.

The carriage slowed again, and as she glanced out the window, she saw the Larnwick's townhouse loom above them. Candles and torches were blazing outside, footmen in livery genially welcoming guests who were queuing—actually queuing!—to go in.

Steeling herself for the evening that was to come; Emerald took another deep breath—but then started.

Instead of slowing to a complete stop and waiting in line with the other carriages, as she had expected, the carriage instead sped up. Sped up so quickly, in fact, that they had left the street within a moment, before Emerald could say a thing.

What was going on?

She turned, instinctively to Robert. "I don't understand."

He had a knowing smile. "You really think we would have gone to the ball?"

Emerald blinked. "Well—yes."

Why else were they here, after all? Was that not the agreement with her mother; had not Opal been clear that the Larnwicks' ball would complete their compromise, releasing her from ever having to attend a ball again?

But Robert was shaking his head, his handsome smile calming her fractured nerves. "Emerald, you are wonderful. You hate balls, hate them with a passion—I would even go so far as to say you loathe them."

She had to smile.

"I do indeed," she admitted with a smile. "But you knew that from the first moment you set eyes on me. That does not explain why we are not attending the ball tonight."

"Well," said Robert delicately, "I thought this evening could be better spent."

Emerald raised an eyebrow. Was the man really so...well. Hungry for her? Could he not wait the few more weeks before they were husband and wife?

"Robert," she said. "Can you really not keep your hands off me until the wedding?"

"I did not mean that!" laughed Robert, though one of his hands escaped hers and reached around her waist, pulling her closer. "Though now you come to mention it..."

Emerald welcomed his passionate kiss, losing herself in the intimacy and pleasure she now entirely associated with the man beside her.

When the kiss finally broke, she was breathless, tingling with desire, and half disappointed now he had not meant that.

"Better spent," Emerald repeated, eyes hazy with lust. "What do you mean, better spent?"

The carriage rattled along, and as she glanced at the window, she was surprised to see that she did not recognize where they were. This was unusual, having lived in London all her life, there were few places in the city she did not know.

Emerald rather thought that they had left London.

Green fields could be seen in the distance, cottages rather than townhouses littered the skyline, and was that—was that a cow?

"I thought," said Robert quietly, "instead of making you stand in a hot room listening to dull people attempt to wrangle gossip from your lips, you might want to see...my home. Your home, before long."

Emerald's heart leapt. "Truly?"

Robert's home—their home. A place in the country, a place where they could be alone together, lost in nature, far from the prying eyes of those who would wish to make mischief. A home that would be hers, and hers alone, no sharing with sisters or waiting to be told what to do by her mother.

*Their home.*

Robert nodded. "I know it is probably highly irregular that I take you with me like this, but—"

"You think it possible for us to generate more gossip?" asked Emerald wryly. "Why, Lady Romeril herself told me—"

Her future husband groaned. "Oh no, what did she say?"

She had to laugh. Well, she knew how Lady Romeril could inspire fear in even the boldest of men, but her mother's friend and her sister's godmother had been rather direct in her advice to Emerald.

"Marry him," Lady Romeril had advised, not that her advice had actually been sought. "Marry him as soon as possible."

And Emerald had laughed, a little nervously, and replied, "I am engaged to be married to him, your ladyship."

And Lady Romeril had frowned, put out, and said, "Without my encouragement?"

"Lady Romeril," Emerald replied as the carriage slowed, turning into a drive she could barely make out in the growing gloom, "was rather complimentary about you."

"Lady Romeril," said Robert dryly, "once told me she never had time to waste on wastrels, nor the desire to tell the undesirable where to go."

It was impossible not to laugh at such words. "I can believe that."

But Emerald did not wish to talk about Lady Romeril at the moment, not when her eyes were feasting on the sights before her. A lawn—stretches of lawn, what looked like formal gardens in the distance…and was that a herd of deer in the background?

"Welcome," murmured Robert in her ear, "to Dellamore Lodge."

Emerald stared. A small place in the country, he had called it. There had been no expectations of grandeur, no promises of wealth—besides, it had always been her sister Coral who had been so focused on riches. But this?

A great Tudor manor house emerged from the growing dusk, with spires, chimneys, and dramatic large windows reflecting the dying rays of the sun. Two tall columns stood on either side of the tall double front doors, all oak and iron knobs.

It was magnificent.

"Are you sure you live here?" breathed Emerald.

There was a chuckle beside her. "You aren't impressed?"

"Too impressed, I think," she said quietly, heart racing a little.

And she was to be mistress of all this? She was to consider this her home, order about the servants, perhaps even welcome visitors?

Her heart twisted as the carriage pulled up by the striking doors. The driver stepped to the door, stepping back to allow Robert to descend. Then the Marquess of Swindmore offered out his hand.

"Emerald?"

Emerald took a deep breath before taking his hand and stepping out of the carriage. There was a rather sacrilegious feeling to the visit, as though she should have been welcomed here for the first time on their wedding day, or after their wedding journey to the Lakes. Her parents had spoken of it so fondly over the years, she quite longed to see it.

But this place, this future home of hers, was beautiful.

"It's very out of the way," she breathed.

It was not the right thing to say; she could see that the moment she glanced into Robert's eyes. Was that hurt there? Was she not effusive enough about her future home?

"But it's very pretty," Emerald added hastily. "Beautiful, even—"

"You don't mind that it is so isolated?" Robert asked quietly. "It's but twenty minutes to Town, but I rather like being out here on my own."

Emerald smiled. That, she could well believe. "I never thought I would find somewhere so convenient, yet so entirely set apart from anyone else."

"That," Robert said, "is precisely why I thought you would like it."

She chuckled quietly. There was no sound on the light breeze, nothing that indicated there was another human within a hundred miles.

"But what about when someone builds a home? There, that prospect, that would make a charming location for a home."

Robert looked where she was pointing. "Perhaps so, but no one will ever build there."

Emerald frowned. "Fortune teller now, are you?"

"Owner and proprietor," came the gentle reply.

Her mouth fell open as she tried to take in everything that simple statement contained. "You mean—you cannot possibly mean that all this land is…is yours?"

She looked around again, trying to comprehend what Robert had said. Owner and proprietor. All of this land, as far as the eye could see…it was all his?

"You are a mighty landlord," Emerald breathed.

Robert snorted. "I don't suppose my land agent appreciates the fact that I do nothing with it, mind you. Most of it is deer land, I have a little woodland that I like to keep maintained—there's a canal further on, I permit a few people to use—"

"But other than that…we are alone?"

Robert pulled Emerald into his arms, and she willingly succumbed to his embrace. "I wanted you to see this, before the wedding—"

"You could have mentioned—"

"Because I wanted you to know that committing to a life with me, as my marchioness, doesn't have to be hosting balls and tea parties and giving concerts and being seen in all the right places," said Robert with a wry smile. "I don't want that sort of wife. I don't want that sort of life. I just want you."

Emerald could have burst with love for him. Each day she discovered new depths to this man.

A life with Robert here in the country without any fuss.

"What about Town?"

He shrugged. "What about it?"

"Robert!"

"If we need to be seen at anything in particular, I will go and you can stay here," he said more seriously. "I can suffer Town quite easily, and you can't. So, don't. Be happy here."

Emerald could hardly believe such happiness existed. What had she done to deserve, to earn such contentment?

"I love you," she said, still a little shyly, the words still uncommon on her tongue. "You do know that, don't you, Robert? I love you—I am more in love with you every single day."

"And you will tell me, won't you?" Robert said, anxiety painted across his brows. "If you—you ever tire of me, or need something more from me, or—"

Emerald stopped up his mouth with a passionate kiss, her hands grasping at the lapels of his jacket to bring him closer.

Tire of him?

As her lips parted to welcome him in, Emerald abandoned herself to the kiss, to him, to all the promise that he offered.

"Robert Ainsworth," she said, breathless after minutes of passionate kisses. "I will never tire of you. I will never leave you. I will always love you."

She could see how much he needed to hear those words, to know he was adored, and Emerald loved that about him. A man who could be honest, could be as shy as she was about some things…who would not want a man like that?

"Though I must tell you," Emerald added, after a moment's thought, "I will need to go into Town in a month or so."

Robert groaned. "I have only just managed to get you out of there, and now you're telling me you want to go back?"

She laughed at that, adoring the sensation of being in his

arms, of standing out here by their home, the place where they would be so happy.

"I do apologize, I am sure," Emerald said with a mock haughtiness in her tone. "But I believe that in six weeks or so, it will be necessary to see Dr. Walsingham, and—"

"Doctor?" Robert pushed her back to look into her eyes, real panic in his voice now. "You are unwell?"

"I am about to be very unwell indeed," Emerald said wryly. "And then…and then nothing will ever be the same again, and everything will be wonderful."

He did not understand. She could see he did not understand, and that made the moments before revealing everything all the more wonderful.

Emerald could feel joy rushing through her veins, and she could hardly believe that she could be so happy—that she would make someone else so happy with just a few simple words.

But he did not know yet. Robert frowned, gripping her arms now as he said slowly, "You're not making any sense, Emerald. What could possibly—"

"We're going to have a baby," Emerald said in a rush.

For a moment, she wondered whether she had been too hasty. Robert stared, his fingers still gripping her arms, his eyes blank and his jaw slack.

Then something happened Emerald had never expected. A tear fell down one of his cheeks.

"Truly?" Robert breathed.

Emerald swallowed, emotion suddenly robbing her almost completely of speech. "As sure as I can be—my flux was missed, completely, and I have never before—and I have been so nauseous, my mother once said she was never so sick as when she was carrying me, and—"

"A baby," Robert breathed in wonder.

As he pulled her into a tight embrace, Emerald wished it would never end. In that moment, all their hopes came together in the idea of one thing: a child. A child of theirs. Part him and part her.

And then Robert was releasing her, laughing gruffly, and dashing away the tears in his eyes. "You must think me a fool."

"You are passionate and wonderful, and a father by this time next year," Emerald said impulsively, her heart thumping wildly. "We will just have to hope that if we have a daughter, she is more like her aunts!"

Robert kissed her swiftly, then looked deep into her eyes. "As long as she turns out like her mother, a contrary debutante to the hilt, I will be very content indeed."

# EPILOGUE

*July 18, 1810*

MICAH...

It was outrageous.

Insulting.

And worst of all, it was his own family.

"What?" said Coral defensively. "All I said was—"

"I know perfectly well what you said," snapped Micah, hackles rising, desperately wishing to escape this ridiculous charade of family respectability. "And I wish you would not repeat it."

"But I only said—"

"Damnit, Coral!"

Micah winced. He had not intended to speak so loudly, the church still filling up with people. Its interior, perfectly designed to amplify any sound made within it, echoed with his badly timed rudeness.

*"Damnit Coral...damnit Coral..."*

His sister's cheeks were flushed. "How dare you! On Emerald's wedding day, the least you could do was—"

"Coral, tell me about these decorations you helped with," said her husband swiftly.

Micah shot his brother-in-law a look of gratitude. At least this duke who was daft enough to marry into the de Petras family was good for something.

But for some reason, Edward did not return his smile. Quite on the contrary, his smile was perfunctory at best, and though he distracted the incensed woman, Micah was left with the rather inconvenient sensation he had been in the wrong.

Which was ridiculous. It was Coral who had spoken so rudely.

"You should not provoke her, dear," said their mother, Opal, placidly.

Micah bristled as he sat in the front pew of the church. "Oh, of course, you take her side! She was the one who—"

"Two wrongs don't make a right, Micah," said his little sister, Sapphire, with that wicked grin she always had whenever about to stir trouble.

Micah stuck his tongue out, Sapphire followed suit, but their mother only saw—

"Micah!"

With a heavy sigh, Micah crossed his arms and sat tetchily in the pew, listening to the growing chatter as the church filled up.

He'd said from the beginning, Emerald would hate this. Why, the woman wouldn't say boo to a goose. The last thing she'd want was a church full of gossiping, sniping Society, ready to criticize her wedding gown, the flowers, the choice of music, the husband himself...

Micah shook his head. *A divorced man!* Well, there appeared to be no harm in him, and he had actually met quite a few people who had been divorced, one way or another. Remarkably pleasant people.

But still. Emerald hated gossip, didn't she? Hated attention. Why, Micah could hardly remember a time when his middle sister had not attempted to avoid all notice whatsoever.

And now she was not only marrying a divorced man, but one who was a marquess?

"I really thought I should give her away," his mother was murmuring to a pacified Coral, who nevertheless took the opportunity to glower at her brother. "After all, I did not give you away…"

Micah gritted his teeth. If his mother had insisted on giving away Emerald, when she knew full well that Society's expectations were that their father did it, he would have refused to come to the wedding, Emerald's feelings be damned.

Was it not enough that the entire family was gawked at wherever they went, with a woman heading it? Had he not received enough ribbing from his university friends, now merely acquaintances as their friendship grew too painful, about how it was Coral and not himself who was the heir?

"Oh, Micah, not this again," sighed Opal.

Micah glared at his mother. "Easy for you to say, you never had to—"

"This is not the place," snapped Coral. "When you are ready to have a reasonable conversation about it, we can—"

"Emerald will be here any moment," Sapphire said quietly.

That was enough to calm the family—at least, in the main. Micah could still feel his temper prickling under the surface, raised but given no satisfaction.

"I thought you said you had invited a guest, Micah?" asked his little sister.

A rather mischievous grin crept across Micah's face, leading to an immediate groan from his mother.

"Micah, what have you done?"

"So quick to assume the worst, aren't you?" he shot back, though shame tightened around his heart. If the shoe fit… "Besides, she hasn't arrived, maybe she thought better—ah, here she is."

Micah had turned as he spoke toward the open church doorway, and in a rush of silks and linen, the entire de Petras family turned.

A wicked smile crept across his face. Well, there was nothing like a wedding to bring the most ridiculous sense of style out of Annie, but even he had to admit, this was a bit much, even for a marquess's wedding.

Absolutely dripping in diamonds and wearing a silk bonnet wider than she was, Annie was drawing attention with every step she took. Her pelisse was hemmed with gold silk, gold silk that matched the large parasol she still had open on her shoulder, and a dark rouge tinted both lips and cheeks.

"Annie," Micah said happily.

"Micah!" hissed Sapphire, eyes wide. "You...you invited your mistress?"

*Mistress was a strong word.* He had not actually made any formal arrangements with Annie. He bedded her most Wednesdays, paid her a little, and that was all.

Mistress. What a formal idea. Though, yes, he supposed in a certain light—

"Mistress?" repeated Coral in horror. "Micah, you didn't!"

"I was told I could invite a guest," Micah said, delighted as Annie made her way slowly down the aisle toward them, evidently luxuriating in the attention she was receiving. How unlike his sister she was. "A guest, you said, and—"

"When I said you could invite a guest, I had thought you would invite that lovely Miss Howarth you were found on the stairs with," Opal de Petras said in an undertone without taking a breath. "Not a harlot who couldn't find her own innocence if—"

"You have gone too far this time," said Sapphire quietly.

Micah's smile did not flicker. He would not give them the satisfaction.

"You are impossible," Coral said irritably as Annie reached the pew and beamed. "Hullo."

"Good morning, and thank you for inviting me," fluttered Annie, curtseying low.

Micah watched as his family stood, unsure precisely how to greet her. His mother nodded her head, as though that was sufficient, and Coral merely glared.

Sapphire leaned forward. "Is that rouge?"

"Sapphy!" Micah hissed. Really, the girl knew nothing of

decorum.

Annie grinned. "Budge up, I'll tell you all about it. Lord, what happened to your arm?"

"Nothing," said Sapphire calmly, moving up the pew so Micah's mistress could join her.

Opal raised her eyes to high heaven. "You have gone too far this time."

Micah grinned. If anything, he had not gone far enough. Why, with the four women he was currently frequenting, he could have had almost a full pew of them. Now that would give the gossips of London something to talk about...

"She is going to be here any moment," his mother was saying in a low tone, shooting his mistress an outraged glance. "Emerald will not appreciate seeing a woman like that—"

"Annie has every right to be here as my guest," interrupted Micah. "And I think Emerald will be delighted—think how many column inches my mistress will get, no one will be looking at—"

"No one will be looking at her on her wedding day?"

"Don't say mistress in church, Micah!"

Micah sighed as his family continued to rail at him.

"Micah, there you are. I wondered where you were this morning," came a deep voice from the end of the nave.

The de Petras family turned once more, and Micah saw his mother relax the instant she saw her husband.

Micah, however, groaned. Jasper de Petras was all very well as a father, of course, but he did insist in attempting to...well. Improve him. It was most provoking. Could not a man be middling and happy about it?

Jasper strode up the nave, holding a piece of paper without Emerald on his arm.

A prickle of uncertainty rushed up Micah's spine. *Where was she?* Had she finally given into the nerves this wedding day had been growing in her, and decided to call the whole thing off?

"She's bolted," he said the moment his father joined them.

"Micah!" That was his mother again. "Don't even say such

a—"

"She has," said Jasper heavily.

Micah's mouth fell open. He had said it as a jest, a tease to provoke his mother and sisters—but never had he believed Emerald would actually do such a thing.

Why, she had seemed absolutely besotted with the man! It was Robert this and Robert that…Micah had even forgotten last week's family dinner so he would not be forced to endure another monologue about their improvements for his country seat.

It was unlike Emerald, but there it was. Love appeared to do strange things to people.

Micah shivered. *All the more reason to avoid it.*

"Emerald's canceling the wedding?" Sapphire breathed, eyes agog.

"Who's Emerald?" asked Annie with a beaming smile.

Micah rolled his eyes. That was the trouble with Annie. *Pretty yes, but no brains.* "My sister. The bride."

"The bride?" Annie frowned. "She cannot cancel the wedding, with no wedding, there ain't no marriage."

"I don't think that would have made much difference," cut in Jasper, and for some reason, Micah did not understand, he was smiling. "Here."

He handed the piece of paper to his wife, and Opal grabbed it and quickly scanned its contents. Her mouth fell open. She handed it to Coral—*of course it went to Coral next*, thought Micah bitterly—who read it in turn, her husband reading it over her shoulder.

The two of them had the same reaction. "No!"

"Yes," said Jasper heavily.

"What is it?" asked Micah.

Sapphire pulled the paper from her sister's hand and started to read it.

Micah's blood began to boil. Was he always to be last in this family—always the bottom of the pile, the very last rung? Was he truly the last to know?

"Well, spit it out, Sapphy," he snapped.

Sapphire looked up from the paper with a grin. "They've eloped."

"Eloped?" Micah repeated. "Emerald?"

It made sense, of course. She hated crowds, hated attention, hated so much of what a wedding was…it was a wonder he had not thought about it before.

"Eloped!" Opal wailed, the word echoing around the church. "Eloped!"

Frantic murmurs now rushed around the church, the word repeated over and over again as weddings guests bowed their heads to share thoughts with their fellows.

"I always thought she would—"

"So unlike her!"

"Did you ever meet her? I know the marquess, never heard of this Miss Emerald de Petras—"

Micah could not help but grin. *Well played, Ems, well played. Get us all at the church, out of the house, ready for a wedding that probably cost an arm and a leg but drew all our attention here…*

Then slip into a carriage, quick as you like, off to Scotland.

He had to applaud her. She had done something Coral had never done, and that was disappoint their mother—something he could see quite plainly in Opal's face.

"Eloped," repeated Opal, her face crestfallen. "Oh, Emerald! Wed without her mother, without any of her family—"

"She'll love it," said Jasper dryly. "Two witnesses, neither of whom know her? She'll be in her element."

"It certainly seems to be more Emerald's style," Sapphire pointed out.

"And by the by, my dear," their father said, dropping his voice so that only Opal and Micah could hear him, "Emerald left a second note I thought best not to bring to church—something about needing a doctor when she returned. She said you'd understand."

Micah glanced at his mother. A doctor? Surely that would only increase his mother's anxiety, not calm it.

Opal's mouth fell open. "A doctor? A doctor, but the only reason she would…she was asking about…Emerald!"

Micah could not follow this. It was all code women seemed to know and men were kept firmly out of, but such a radiant smile had spread across his mother's face. It appeared to be good news. He breathed a sigh of relief. This would calm their mother, knowing that this elopement would make her daughter happy should, naturally, be precisely what she wanted.

But it was Coral who seemed the most put out by the revelation that Emerald would not be trotting down the aisle before them any time soon. "But the expense! The tremendous expense for the church, the flowers, the reception—"

"Oh, Coral, no one cares about the money," Micah snapped, pushed beyond all endurance. Was this what his family was? Penny pinchers who cared more about the look of the thing than whether Emerald was happy? "You just care because you get to play at the heir!"

"And you're just put out because you can't!" Coral shot back.

Micah stood up. He'd had enough of this. What if he'd actually felt something for Annie, eh? He had to stifle a laugh at the next passing thought; what if he'd wanted to marry her?

Well, if his family were not going to show Emerald or Annie any respect, he saw no reason to stay.

"Micah?" Opal said blankly. "Where are—"

"Well, it's not like there's going to be a wedding, is there?" pointed out Micah bad-temperedly. The sooner he could get out of here… "So, I thought I would go and have some actual fun. Come on, Annie."

"Micah!"

"Not like that," he added hurriedly at his mother's outrage.

Goodness gracious, he may be a rake and a cad, but he was not so foolish to suggest that sort of thing while standing in a church.

Though, as Annie rose obediently and took his arm, finding some fun in the arms of a woman was not the worst idea. Not Annie, though. Was Catherine around this afternoon?

"Micah, when will we see you next?"

It was Sapphire who asked. Micah turned round for a moment to see her standing in the nave, looking back at him, concern lined across her face.

It should have made him feel guilty, he knew, but guilt was an emotion he had not felt in a long time. What did he have to feel guilty for? He did what he liked, spent what he liked, had taken rooms years ago so he did not have to stay in his parents' house within their rules…

Guilt simply did not come into the picture.

"You'll see me next when I decide you will," Micah said with a heavy sigh. "I can't keep dancing to this de Petras tune. I have my mistresses to keep me company, and that's enough."

And with that, he strode out of the church with one mistress on his arm, but an entirely different one in his heart…

**Discover which mistress Micah has in his heart—and just whether she'll ever truly turn his head—in The Determined Mistress…Book 4 of THE DE PETRAS SAGA.**

# About Emily E K Murdoch

If you love falling in love, then you've come to the right place.

I am a historian and writer and have a varied career to date: from examining medieval manuscripts to designing museum exhibitions, to working as a researcher for the BBC to working for the National Trust.

My books range from England 1050 to Texas 1848, and I can't wait for you to fall in love with my heroes and heroines!

Follow me on twitter and instagram @emilyekmurdoch, find me on facebook at facebook.com/theemilyekmurdoch, and read my blog at www.emilyekmurdoch.com.